HEART *of the* WITCH, SOUL *of the* WOLF

Brenda Bassett

Heart of the Witch, Soul of the Wolf

Brenda Bassett

ISBN: 979-8-35093-916-3

1

Three sisters sat in rocking chairs around a fire outside their small farmhouse, somewhere in the Yucatan, enjoying a cooling breeze after a sweltering day. The night sky was clear and starry. They lived very near the Mayan ruins of Uxmal, or, as the locals called it, El Adivino; Pyramid of the Magician. The sisters were Maya and direct descendants of high priests and priestesses who were once the controlling forces of magic in that temple and others nearby. These women were very powerful brujas who were still connected to their ancient ancestors. Just as their ancestors did, they studied the stars on nights like these, looking for messages of the future. This evening the sky was very revealing.

"Maria, do you see the story being told tonight?" asked one of the sisters.

"Si, such strangeness; a foreigner from such a strange country. Their power is very old, like ours. I see the one who will hold all their knowledge within herself. That is a very clever way to preserve their craft; very burdensome for the girl, don't you think Izchel?" asked Maria.

"I wouldn't want to carry that weight around on my shoulders. How very unusual," said Lucia, the third sister, " She will come across the sea, heal the wolf and destroy the reign of La Madre. That makes me very happy. She has been a scourge on our people and she will only get worse. That woman spreads her violence like a plague. She teaches our men and our children to be criminals and murderers. She spreads her death and filth all around us. She is just another lowlife dictator and the gods know we have enough of those to go around in this country. Let's hope the vision comes to fruition but anything can happen, you know."

"My neck hurts from looking up" said Izchel and reached her hand out to the black canvas of stars. Into her hand came down the stars that were telling the sisters the story of what was to come. Izchel motioned her hand to the fire, it flared and the stars began to circle a few feet above it. "That's better. Oh no, poor, poor Valentina."

"Be quiet, you trouble maker," hissed Maria.

Sitting on the porch, away from the fire was a young, pregnant woman rocking her little son as he slept peacefully wrapped in a blanket in her arms. She got up, put her little boy down on a small cot and walked over to the sisters.

"What do you see, Auntie," she asked.

The sisters exchanged troubled glances. Maria had hoped Valentina had not heard her sister's loud mouth.

"The stars are telling a sad story. They say that La Madre will be a source of great pain for you, my poor child," Izchel told her in a very sympathetic tone.

"She has been this for us all, has she not, Auntie. My cousin has no connection to me, why would she hurt me directly?"

"There will be actions set in motion and through her cruelty you will be damaged most severely. All you will have left to live for is revenge and you will have it. The wolf will bring her downfall from the house of light beyond the seas. This is all I can tell you, my child."

Valentina watched the fire for a moment trying to see the stars her aunt had put on display. Sometimes she could see the stories that the stars told, but not tonight. She tried to make sense of the wolf and the house of light. Her aunts always talked in riddles this way and it was never until after the fact that people would realize that the sisters had foretold the future with great accuracy. Valentina thought that her aunts were cryptic on purpose because they liked to see people strain themselves trying to understand the message. She walked slowly back to her son, deciding that she was going to take what they said with a grain of salt; they were very old, after all. As she picked her son up she felt an ice cold chill rush through her. She looked back over her shoulder at the sisters, who were watching her. She saw looks of anguish on their faces. She hugged her son tightly then ran into the small house.

"Some nights it does not pay to see the stars," said Izchel.

"La Madre," said Lucia and spat on the ground in front of the fire

2

A white jeep slowly rolled into a small town during the afternoon heat. Because of the heat there was not much happening. There were some women pressing corn into corn meal and making tortillas and a few others preparing tamales that would be cooked in a pit under the soil. Sitting in front of the cantina was a group of men smoking cigars, drinking tequila, fanning themselves with their hats and playing cards. A little boy braved the heat to kick a soccer ball around the dried out well in the center of the town.

Inside the jeep, there was a nervous tension as the passengers began to gather suspicious, not so friendly looks, from the people watching them enter. The ten year old boy in the jeep wanted out. Once he spied the small boy with the soccer ball, he really wanted to escape the vehicle that seemed to be smothering him with whatever had gotten his father, brother and uncle so tense. He tugged on his fathers arm and whispered to him.

"Papa, can I go play?"

His father had been warily eyeing the men on the porch of the cantina and now scanned across the street to see the boy playing with his ball.

"Si, Javier, go play. Stay near the well." The boy quickly turned and struggled with the car door. His father grabbed him by the arm before he could jump out.

"Javi, listen to me, if you hear any noise, you run back here and hide under the seat and do not make a sound. Do you understand me?"

"Si papa," he replied as he absorbed the seriousness of his father's tone. In an instant he was on the ground with his foot on the soccer ball, feeling all the tension disappear.

Don Arturo exited his vehicle with his oldest son, Gabriel, close behind him. They seemed to be noticed by everyone except the group of men on the porch. Arturo noticed the men at either end of the cantina who were doing a bad job at trying not to be obvious while guarding the group. He signaled to Gabriel with the slightest tilt of his head at them. They walked up the three stairs. Arturo turned an empty chair around, straddled it and leaned his forearms over the back.

"Buenos dias Don Pascal," said Don Arturo.

"Rodrigo! This is a surprise. Is your wife having you run her errands now? What would my Goddaughter demand of me this time? Would she like half of my evening meal or half of these card winnings?" he pointed to the table in front of him. " Why not? She has divided every-thing that was once whole! You do know what happens to a machine with only half its parts, Rodrigo? It cannot run!" Don Pascal slammed his hand down in the middle of the table and swiped away half of the cards, bills and coins to the ground.

"Don Pascal, if you are done being overly dramatic, I will tell you that I have come here to try and soothe the wounds that my wife has, rightfully, inflicted. Not to encourage your sarcasm, but I have come here of my own accord. I would like for you to be able to see the reason behind her actions. She has only taken what her father, your brother, wanted her to have. You know this is her right." This had sounded good to Don Arturo when he was practicing it in his head, but now he was not sure any of what he had to say was going to be soothing.

"Yes, her right, but not what is right!" Don Pascal exclaimed, "and why does she do these things; to prove that she can throw her weight around?!"

"To prove that she has new ways and more strength behind her now than any of us has ever had! Your brother has been dead twelve months. She gave you six months to see what you could do on your own, and what? Nothing! Stagnation! Since she has taken over, she has tripled our profits and has obtained connections you would never have dreamed of!" Don Arturo yelled back; his role as a peaceful negotiator in jeopardy.

Don Pascal sat back in his chair and swallowed a glass of tequila and fanned himself with his hat.

"She is going to get us all killed, Rodrigo. You know this. Maybe not herself, but definitely you and I... and your sons. Do you think she cares what happens to them? She would devour them if she were hungry! I don't know what has happened to you, Rodrigo. You are a smart, clever man. You are loyal and you love your children. By letting her do what she is doing; all I can think is that you have seen the beast inside her and you fear it. Well, Rodrigo, I don't fear it. I do not intend to follow it to hell. But, I do intend to hurt it!" He leaped at Rodrigo.

Don Arturo was about to speak, when he felt a sharp pain in his chest. For a moment he thought he was having a heart attack. He looked across the table at Don Pascal who had a crazed, victorious look in his eyes. Rodrigo felt, smelled and tasted blood as it flowed over his lips and into his hand. For a few seconds, he heard no sound. As his hearing slowly came back, he heard gunfire and Gabriel screaming at him to run. Still locked in Don Pascals' gaze, Rodrigo fell, dead, onto the table.

Gabriel was now running towards his little brother, Javier, who was standing near the well, frozen in terror as he clutched the soccer ball. Their Uncle Francisco had strategically placed himself between the jeep and the cantina and was returning fire at the men on the porch as Gabriel raced past him. Gabriel, ten feet away from his brother, reached out to him but stopped in his tracks. Blood splashed in Javier's face and dripped down his cheeks, mixing with his tears, his ball splashed with blood as well. The little boy behind him crouched next to the well with his hands over his ears and screamed. Uncle Francisco picked Javier up and flung him into the jeep, returning fire as he did.

"Get down and stay down!" he shouted. Javier clutched the soccer ball and buried himself under bags and junk that were on the floor of the jeep. He could hear nothing but the ringing in his ears and feel only the cold wetness of his brother's blood.

3

A few hours later Javier and his uncle arrived home. Francisco got out of the jeep, opened the back door and pulled Javier out of his hiding place. This time Javier did not want to get out of the vehicle. Everyone was coming out of the house. Javier saw all of his mother's men standing at the ready with their machine guns. Then, he saw his mother parting through them like a knife. His uncle ran up to her and grabbed her. He whispered something to her and she fell, limp, in his arms. Javier was watching this scene intently. He started to hear a sound that seemed to make the ground vibrate and he was afraid that the earth beneath them all was about to open up and swallow them whole. This sound, he realized, was coming from his mother and was now turning into a scream. Never before had there been a sound made like that in this world, he was sure. The noise stopped abruptly. Javier's mother pushed away from his uncle and locked eyes with Javier. She was the fire of hell. She was going to burn him to cinder where he stood. He hid his face in the ball; it was his only defense. A maid, who had been Javier's nanny since he was born, jumped in front of him.

"Run Javi! Go to your room and lock the door!" He felt paralyzed but he willed his legs to move and he ran as fast as he had ever run before. Before going into the house Javier looked back to see his mother beating the maid with bare, bloody hands as she made that sound again.

Later that night Javier's mother had come to his room. He had been sitting in the middle of his bed, in the dark, holding the soccer ball and praying to God that his mother would forget about him. The locked door opened effortlessly and Javier thought to himself, what an illusion of safety that lock was. He heard the clicking of her high heels against the marble tiled floor coming towards him. She sat on the bed next to him and spoke to him with a voice, raspy from screaming.

"My son, mi amore, we are all alone now. You will stay by my side and become my protector. You are the man of the house now. You must be brave and strong. Will you do this for me?"

"Si mama." he answered, trying not to sound like he had been crying for hours.

"Do you want mama to show you how to be strong, to be danger-ous, to be loyal to your family?" she asked him.

"Yes mama," a little stronger this time.

His mother put her hand on the ball and looked at it attentively.

" What a wonderful ball. Where did you get it?"

"From a boy in the village where…" He looked up swiftly at his mother, in terror when he realized what he almost said to her.

"Were you playing soccer with a little boy in the village when… it happened?" his mother asked, sounding very strained.

"Si, mama," he answered in a whisper. Of course she already knew every detail of what happened and she was here to interrogate him.

"Do you think your little friend will want his ball back? You will not have time to play ball now that you are the man of this house. You will have many duties. We will go to the village tomorrow and give the boy back his ball. I have sent men to the village to… take care of things, and I will want to see how they did. This will also give me a chance to teach you some things; to help you in your new position in this family."

Javier was very puzzled. He was sure the first thing his mother was going to do when she had come to this room would be to beat him to death. He was, also, still trying to figure out why that would be. It seemed that it was impossible to figure out what drew her wrath. Sometimes it seemed that she just waited to be angry at him. He was shocked that she was sitting with him now, making plans for his future. A few minutes ago he didn't think he had one. Now she wanted to return the ball to a boy, Javier was sure, his mother considered to be a peasant. Why would she even be thinking about this? Javier figured she wanted to take the ball from him because, somehow, she knew that this ball was the only thing comforting him. This was how she would punish him; again, for what he did not know. Trying to think some steps ahead of his mother was something Javier had learned to do for self preservation. Sometimes it helped, but usually she was just too many steps ahead of him.

His mother got up and started toward the door. She did not help him get under the covers or say good night to him. His nanny usually did that, but Javier did not want to think of that now. His mind could not process that on top of the day's traumatic events. A kiss goodnight from his mother was the stuff his nanny told him about in fairy tales.

"Mama, can I have a bath before I go to sleep?" he asked as he inhaled the smell of the dry blood that still covered him.

"I will send the maid up in the morning. Your sleep is more important right now and the blood will help you to dream of your father and brother tonight." she replied; as if he would be able to dream of anything else. His father's lifeless body being kicked down the cantina stairs and his brother's face, stunned as he was shot in the back, is all

Javier could see when he closed his eyes. He continued to cry silently after his mother left the room, until exhaustion took him.

The next day would have been like any other except for the absence of the three people who had shaped Javier's life up to this point; his father, brother and nanny. Had they been here, the day would have had the possibility of some laughter or some fun and maybe some sign of love. Sometimes mother would show love towards father but that would always be short lived. Today, his mother sat at one end of the table and Javier sat at the other, in the chair his father would have sat in. They sat silently eating breakfast. After that, Javier and his mother were driven to the village. There were three jeeps in front of them and three behind them. The vehicles piled into the village and when the dust settled, Javier saw many men with guns. At first, he began to feel that, now, all too familiar feeling of terror well up in his stomach; but then he realized that the men were his mother's men. Javier recognized the men from the cantina. They were on their knees with their hands behind their heads. Some of his mother's men were pointing their machine guns at them. One of the men on his knees was his mother's uncle, Don Pascal. He was badly beaten. Javier's mother got out of the jeep and walked over to Don Pascal. He straightened as tall as he could and said some things to her. He looked very proud and defiant. Javier feared for him.

After staring at the men for a few minutes, she turned around and walked back to the jeep. She opened the door for Javier to get out and took him by the hand. He held the soccer ball under his other arm. His mother walked him over towards the well and turned to face him.

"Is this where you were playing with your little friend yesterday?" she asked.

"Si, mama," he answered as his mother nodded at one of the men who brought the little boy over to them. She turned to the small child and knelt down in front of him.

"Hello little one. Your friend, Javier, has come to bring your soccer ball back to you; haven't you Javier? Show him." Javier held out the blood spattered ball. The little boy smiled a big smile, which was more than Javier had the courage to do. Javier realized that the boy couldn't be more than five years old, which was probably why he was not paying attention to the situation surrounding him. Before the boy could grab his ball, Javier's mother swooped the little boy up in her arms and sat him on the rim of the well.

"Before we give you your ball back, I have something for you." she said, as she sweetly, motherly swept the hair out of the boy's eyes using her long red fingernails. She pulled a lollipop out of her pocket and gave it to the boy who eagerly grabbed it, opened it and popped it in his mouth. His mother laughed.

"That is my gift to you for letting my son borrow your wonderful ball," she said to the little boy in the sweetest voice. Javier was in disbelief. His mother had the little boy under a spell. Who was this woman who talked so sweetly and used such kind words and, Dios mio, had candy to give out? Javier also wondered if, maybe, this was a new beginning; maybe this was how his mother would be from now on; now that they only had each other.

"Have you ever had such delicious candy before?" she asked.

The boy shook his head, no.

"Well you enjoy it my little mouse" she said softly as she continued to use her fingernails to stroke his hair. Then she used the palm of her hand on his forehead to casually push him backwards into the well.

There was complete silence. The boy did not have enough time to realize that he was plummeting to his death at the bottom of the well. He did not have enough time to scream. But screams began to come; from a pregnant woman who was trying to run to the well. She was being held back by the men with the guns. She looked like a butterfly being held by its wings. Javier realized that this was the boy's mother. Looking beyond the screaming woman, Javier saw the look of horror on Don Pascal's face, and then he fell to the ground, sobbing. The boy was his grandson.

Javier's mother grabbed her son by the top of his hair and dragged him right up to the well. The soccer ball bounced away. She held his head over the well.

"Do you see what you have done? That is your fault! You killed that woman's baby! He is dead because you played ball with him while you should have been looking out for your father and your brother. That ball was more important to you than your family. Lesson number one: You protect your family before all else! That woman's baby is dead because my baby is dead! Lesson number two: You avenge your family! You make them suffer ten times what we have suffered!" Her voice was the hiss of a serpent. She held his head over the well for what seemed like an eternity. The little boy looked up at him with a halo of blood around his head; his body broken at the bottom of the well. The lollipop was grasped tightly in his little hand.

"Come" his mother said as she dragged Javier by the arm over to the kneeling men. On the way, they passed the pregnant woman. Her face was streaked with dust and tears. Blood trickled down from her scalp, where the man behind her grasped her by the hair. She grabbed his mother's arm.

"Cousin, you will pay for this!" she yelled. "They have seen your end! I know who will put you down, you filthy bitch! She will come and he will bring her" she said as she pointed to Javier. " You know my aunts, cousin! You know they have the sight! They have seen it, they have seen…" The woman stopped moving and her eyes were huge. After a few seconds she let out that sound like the one Javier's mother had made the day before. The woman grabbed her belly and fell to the ground. An old woman rushed over, as fast as she could, to help her as she had gone into labor.

Javier's mother, once again dragged him by his arm, over to where the kneeling men were. She put a large gun in Javier's hand and put the barrel of it on Don Pascal's forehead.

"Avenge your father and brother, Javier! Pull that trigger!" she hissed into his ear.

"It's ok, Javi. You are a good boy. Do what your mother tells you and when I go to heaven I will tell your papa and your brother how much you love them. Forgive me, Javier for taking them from you but know that she made me do it just as she is making you do this now," Don Pascal then closed his eyes in an attempt to make it easier for Javier. Javier's mother stood behind him, she put her arms around him, and put her hands over his small hands. His finger was on the trigger and hers slid over his. She squeezed his finger and the trigger at the same time. Once again, the now familiar feeling of warm blood was upon Javier's face. Don Pascal slumped down at Javier's feet.

"You have done well, my son. Welcome to your new life. You will destroy my enemies. You are my wolf."

4

A young girl with long brown hair stood upon a hill, with the ocean in front of her and a lighthouse behind her. She was chilled to the bone as she was hit over and over with the whip of the wind from the sea. The smell of salt penetrated her nostrils. Even her father's extra large fisherman's coat could not fend off the cold. She would not leave this spot even if she froze to death, she thought to herself. She was determined to see her father's boat appear on the horizon. She would peer over her shoulder every so often to make sure the lighthouse was doing its job.

This trip was a short one. Her father, Errol, had only been gone a week. Sometimes he would be gone for months at a time but that was when he would come home with a great haul. She overheard her father tell her mother that the fish were becoming scarce and the hauls were dwindling. Her mother, Gwenevere, didn't mind that her husband came back early even though it meant less money. The girl could never understand why her mother married a fisherman and agreed to be a lighthouse keeper. She hated the ocean! The only reason she ran the lighthouse was so she could start watching for her husband the minute his boat left the harbor. It helped ease her anxiety a tiny bit.

They lived on the coast of Cornwall, England, in a remote fishing village. The little girl, Danika, wished she lived in the village. At least there would be human contact besides her mother and her pesky, little sister, Liza. Her family lived way out near the beach and way up on the hill. When her father was at sea it was dead boring. Her mother was too busy schooling Liza or being sick with anxiety over her husband at sea. When her father returned from a trip, he would get paid, and they would have a great meal and presents. Her father would stop and get his girls some toys or art supplies for Dani, after he cashed his check. He would bring his wife a case of red wine. When Danika was very little, like her sister, her father would also bring home bottles of whiskey for himself and they would really have a celebration. Her father would pick her up and twirl her around the house, and chase her, and they would fall down, and he would just act so silly. Danika loved it when her father was wild and crazy like that. Now that she was older, she knew that her father had been drunk the whole time he was home with them and would only sober up to go to sea. She knew her mother hated it when he was drunk. After he was fun, he became very mean and that's when he would pay attention to her mother. When Liza was born he stopped drinking completely. He had gone out to sea the day his wife told them they were to have another child. That time he didn't sober up and was lost at sea the whole nine months his wife was pregnant. They had run out of money and food. They only survived thanks to the kindness of the villagers. He had to promise to never drink again or Gwenevere was leaving for good. He hadn't had a drop since.

To occupy herself Dani (as she was called) would draw or paint. When she wasn't doing that she would be bringing home all kinds of stray animals only to be told that a lighthouse was no place for a pet. She loved nothing more than to be out in nature. She explored every inch of the shore and was beginning to venture into the forest. The light and gentle sounds of the forest were soothing compared to the roar of the ocean on the shore, although she loved them both equally.

When Dani had turned thirteen years old a very strange thing happened. She was walking the path along the forest that led from the lighthouse to the village. There was a strange sound of a woman crying deeper in the woods. Dani went into the woods to see if someone needed help. She looked and looked but couldn't find anyone. She was about to give up when she heard whimpering. That was when she saw the hole. She looked into it and found a beautiful deer staring back up at her. The deer scratched its hooves at the wall of the pit. Dani was very puzzled. She knew she heard a woman crying but this deer was the only creature in sight. She didn't have time to think about it. She had to figure out how to get the deer out of the pit before some hunter came by. Dani frantically looked around for something that would help this deer to get out. She spotted a few long tree limbs rotting on the forest floor. She picked some that were still strong, not too heavy but long. She put them diagonally into the pit so they weren't completely to the bottom and stuck them into the wall of the hole. The deer put one hoof up, then the other on the makeshift ramp. It then hoisted itself onto the tree limbs and out of the hole. Dani and the deer were face to face. Dani looked deep into the deer's eyes. They were the lightest shade of gray and they were magical. There were stars and streaks of light in them. The deer stamped its hoof on the ground and Dani snapped out of her trance. She looked down to see what the deer was trying to tell her. She saw a wire wrapped around the deer's ankle. It was probably from the trap that was set. It was cutting through her flesh. Dani wrestled with the wire for a few minutes but finally managed to get it off.

"Thank you, Dani," said the deer and it bolted away.

Danika walked home in shock. Did that deer just speak to her? How could that be possible? She tried to talk herself out of believing that it had happened but she couldn't. She knew that there was some-thing magical about that deer the minute she laid eyes on it. She didn't say a word through dinner then went right to bed. Before she fell asleep she promised herself that she would wait in the woods everyday until she found that deer again! When she slept, she dreamt of stars in the galaxy and comets shooting by, and deer dancing through the sky. She also dreamt of a beautiful lady who's face she could not quite see.

Bright and early Dani jumped out of bed. She put on an old pair of jeans; actually, they were her only pair of jeans. She threw on her dad's old sweater and his old pea coat and a pair of boots. Around there it was just about as cold in the forest as it was on the shore. She ran past her mother and sister, swiping a piece of toast as she went, yelled goodbye then flew out the door. Danika ran all the way down the path to the forest. She carefully observed the brush along the path to try and remember exactly where she had entered the day before. There was the hole in the ground. She peeked over the edge to make sure the deer wasn't in it. She was pretty sure the deer wasn't dumb enough to fall in twice but she looked anyway. She also wanted to make sure nothing else had fallen in. Dani looked around for a place to sit so she could watch the whole area for any signs of life.

About a half hour had gone by and she had observed some tiny birds, a couple of insane squirrels chasing each through the leaves on the forest floor and a busy chipmunk. Dani's fingers were starting to freeze and she was wishing that she hadn't forgotten her gloves. As she blew hot breath on her fingers she heard a voice that came from right behind her.

"What are we looking for, Dani?"

Dani jumped up and spun around. Squatting down where Dani had just been was the beautiful woman from her dream. She was wear-ing a long dark green cloak with a large hood. Dani could see silky, dark auburn hair underneath it. Her skin was milky white and smooth like porcelain. Then, she saw them. Those beautiful light gray eyes!

"It's you." Dani whispered.

"I had to come back to thank you for your help. You were absolutely heroic! So sorry for running off but I was in the middle of trying a new spell when I got caught in that terrible trap and I needed to get right home to reform so I could make a potion to heal my wound."

Danika looked down at the lady's extended ankle. There was a thin cut around it, just like what should be on the deer's leg. Dani felt the urge to slap herself to make sure she was awake. She couldn't believe what she was hearing.

"You were the deer? Now you are a lady? There was a cut on the deer and now it's on you?" Dani sputtered.

"Yes, yes, yes and yes," the woman responded.

"You're a witch!" Dani exclaimed.

"You could say that," said the lady.

"Teach me!" Dani pleaded as she fell to her knees in front of the woman and grabbed the hem of her dress as if not to let it go unless her plea was answered.

"Of course," answered the woman, then asked her "are you free for the afternoon?"

The two young ladies began a long walk, deep into the forest. As they walked they got to know each other.

" How do you know my name?" Dani asked the tall, elegant woman.

"I also know that you live at the lighthouse with your father, Errol, your mother, Gwenevere, and your sister Liza; and that you are an artist and love animals. Did I get it all right?" she asked.

"That is amazing," Dani said, astounded.

"No It's not, silly. I simply asked about you in the village. You are well enough known there. People are very nosy about the people in the lighthouse." laughed the woman.

Danika stopped walking, put her hands on her hips and pouted,

"That's not fair. All I know about you is that you turn into animals; which is entirely more interesting than anything that you know about me. I don't even know your name."

The lady walked back to Dani, put a finger under her chin to lift her head up.

" My name is Jenna Grey and I am very pleased to have made your acquaintance Danika Devlyn. What I don't know about you is, what are your desires? Are you willing to work hard for those desires? Do you believe that you can have anything in the world that you want when you call it to you? Lastly, can you truly understand the power of balance in this world?"

Dani was stumped. She, absolutely, did not know the answers to any of those questions and just stood there feeling dumb. Jenna laughed a lovely, melodic laugh.

"Of course you don't know the answers. These are life altering questions. Most people never ask themselves these kinds of questions and never reach their true potential or obtain their truest desires. I will help you learn these things and we will see where it leads you." She grabbed Dani's hand.

"Run!" she shouted gleefully.

They ran together out of the forest into a clearing towards a small cottage in the distance. Jenna was pulling Dani and laughing. Dani ran faster and started to laugh with her. They ran together, faster and faster and laughed louder and louder. Dani felt a slight suction feeling in the top center of her stomach. It was a feeling she never felt before. It felt wonderful. Dani soon realized that her feet were not touching the ground.

5

Some years passed, and in that time Jenna had become the most important person in Danika's life. She opened doors to Danika that she never would have dreamt existed. She was teaching her ancient magic. Dani spent everyday at Jenna's cottage and some nights when she could get away with it. Dani told her mother that she started going to school in the village and had new friends that she liked to hang out with. It was sort of true. She was in a type of school and there was a friend that she wanted to be with. However, no school in the world could offer her the education she was getting from Jenna, and Dani absorbed it all.

At the cottage the two young ladies had no interruptions. There was an old woman named Ingrid, who lived with Jenna and took care of the busy work. Ingrid was a very powerful witch, Jenna explained. She was hundreds of years old and had been Jenna's teacher since she started in the craft. At this point in her life Ingrid was happy to be a house witch and used the least taxing of her magic to take care of Jenna, the cottage and now, Dani. Dani instantly loved Ingrid. She was the grandmother she never had. Ingrid was plump, with long brown hair that she wore in braids on top of her head. She was so affectionate and thoughtful, taking care of Jenna and Dani's every need. Ingrid did not speak much, however. She said everything she needed to say with her facial expressions. Some days Dani would forget that Ingrid was there. She would do a lot of her work from her chair as she sat silently rocking by the fireplace petting whatever cat would happen to be in her lap; there were dozens around the cottage. The only time she would speak would be to correct Jenna if she was giving Dani the wrong information about a potion or spell and that would always make Jenna blush with embarrassment.

One day Dani asked Jenna, "Why are you teaching me? Do you teach anyone you meet?"

"Only the person I was meant to teach would have found that deer in the forest that day. The fact that you found me when I was in danger was an even greater sign that you were meant to be my pupil. Make no mistake Dani, you are very special. I am teaching you many things and someday I will ask you something in return. But let's not speak of it now. We have work to do"

The ladies went back to bundling dry herbs. Some days, the work could be a little dull. Dani didn't think much of what Jenna may want from her; she trusted her completely.

Dani arrived at the cottage early one morning to find Jenna putting a saddle on her horse.

"Where are we going?" Dani asked.

"Well, I know how much you love an adventure," replied Jenna.

"I don't need an adventure, Jenna. I'd just like to do something besides identifying and picking herbs in the forest. So, what are we going to do?" Dani asked again.

"We are going to travel north east and delve deep into a dark forest,"

"And?" Dani asked impatiently.

"And, identify and pick mushrooms!" Jenna exclaimed.

"Arrrrgh!" Dani cried as she dropped her head down on Jenna's shoulder.

"Come on. You're gonna enjoy this trip. It's a means to an end. Up on Mystery and I'll tell you all about it," Jenna told her.

" Now Danika," Jenna began as they galloped across the field toward the path, " We are going in search of very special mushrooms. We will be looking for blackened hoof mushrooms. They are used in initiation ceremonies. They only grow once every one hundred years and wither in a month, and that's if some forest creature doesn't get it first. The number of mushrooms that grow will determine how many will be initiated into our coven within that time." A mist began to appear where the path began.

"Are we riding into that fog? How will Mystery see where she is going?" Dani asked, nervously.

Jenna replied, "It's a doorway. Mystery has traveled through many doorways. Hold on!"

Right then the beautiful black horse took a giant leap into the mist. The sound of the galloping stopped and Dani felt as if they were floating. That was the only sensation she could feel. She couldn't feel herself breathing; she didn't think her heart was beating. After a few seconds, Mystery landed her jump on a new path. This forest was completely unfamiliar to Dani. It was very old with thick green moss and vines growing everywhere. It looked suffocatingly dense.

"Have you gone in here before?" Dani asked.

"Not too often. This forest, as you can tell, is not too inviting and allows you to take only what is necessary. It doesn't like anyone hanging around too long. If you abuse its hospitality it will let you know about it, so tread lightly and keep your wits about you. There are many magical creatures here and some have their own agendas."

Jenna took Dani by the hand and they entered the forest leaving Mystery on the path to wait for them. Dani was mesmerized. Everything glistened as if every leaf and every limb were coated in sugar. There was a gentle mist and the distant sound of a waterfall. There was an abundance of creatures coming out to see who the visitors were. Frogs jumped back and forth across the small path in front of them. Dani saw snakes sliding along tree limbs. There were ancient standing stones dotting the forest, wearing jackets of the thick moss. The enchantment in this place was so thick Dani could almost taste it. She broke away from Jenna and sat near a stream that looked as if it were glowing. She felt the water with her hand and it made her feel a bit dizzy. She took her hand out and in her palm was a butterfly. She looked closer and saw that its wings were tiny red berries, strung together. The butterfly stretched out its wing as though it were offering some of the berries to her. Dani was about to pick one and taste it but Jenna ran over and shook the creature out of her hand and it flew back into the water.

"Stay focused Danika. One of those berries can kill ten men."

Dani felt a fear rise in her.

"No fear Dani. Respect. Respect is all this place asks for. Stay focused. I see what we are looking for. Come."

Jenna took Dani by the hand and pulled her over to a standing stone with ancient carvings on it. Jenna put her hand on it and closed her eyes. A yellow glow surrounded her hands. The light turned orange then green. Dani began to see mushrooms growing in the moss on the stone. When they were full size she could see that they were brown with a rim of black where the stem connected to the earth.

"Put your hand under them," Jenna told her.

When Dani did this, five mushrooms fell into her palm. The mushrooms were warm. Jenna handed her a piece of silk.

"Wrap them in this and put them in your pocket."

After Dani did this Jenna took out a small knife from her pocket and snipped a small strand of Dani's hair. She held it near the moss that had given the mushrooms. It seemed to reach out and take the lock of hair, caress it, then absorb it.

"It's the balance," Dani whispered.

"Correct," Jenna replied.

Dani knew that she had just witnessed something very sacred.

After the two sat at the foot of the stone for a while they both felt that they had been thanked for their company and were being dismissed. They got up and started to walk back to Mystery.

"So, pilfering my forest again Jenna? Why can't you stay in your own playpen?" said a strange, low voice.

"And miss an opportunity to run into you. Oh, and, it's not your forest Magda, no matter how much you pretend it is."

"Who is your little friend? Oh, don't tell me that this is Ingrid's replacement. She's a little seagull freezing on a buoy." said the woman with her husky voice.

Dani thought the lady said that to her because, somehow, she knew she lived at the lighthouse. She started to feel as if she were rocking on the ocean. She could smell the salt air and hear a bell clanging. Then she started to feel a cold like she had never felt. She felt her lungs freeze and thought her heart was about to stop. She fell to the ground.

"Stop it Magda!" Jenna said as she shoved the woman in the black hooded cloak.

The woman stumbled back a few feet, then let out a childish giggle. The freezing stopped and Dani felt fine but now knew that this woman was no friend. Jenna helped her to her feet then turned to Magda.

"How dare you disrespect the sanctity of this forest. If you want to be a bully, come be a bully out on the path." she threatened.

Dani watched Jenna stand eye to eye with the witch and couldn't believe how intimidating she became; Dani actually became a little frightened herself. The witch backed right down.

"Lucky for you, I've got more important things to do with my time. Some parting words of advice, Jenna. Find a new transfer if that's what you're up to. That one couldn't hold a bowl of marbles, nevermind a sea of knowledge. I didn't take you for the desperate type."

With that, Magda walked behind the standing stone and was gone.

"Well, that was unpleasant but, with her it always is. Are you okay?" Jenna asked.

"I'm okay, I think," Dani replied.

"Good, we got what we game for and we've been here long enough. Let's go home."

They walked out of the forest to find Mystery patiently waiting for them. They rode back through the mist to the cottage. When they were safely home and brushing Mystery down Dani was very quiet.

"What's on your mind, little one?" Jenna asked.

"I'll never doubt you again when you say we're going on an adventure!"

Jenna stared at Dani for a few moments then burst out in hearty laughter which became contagious as Dani joined her. Even Ingrid, who had been listening in while she was collecting eggs from the coup, began to laugh with them as well.

6

Days turned into months, into years. Dani was now sixteen and making great progress in the craft. Everyday's lesson was exhilarating. The more she learned the more connected she became with nature. All the things she already loved, earth, air, fire, water, spirit, were giving her the gift of their secret powers. She grew stronger and stronger and Jenna couldn't have been prouder. Dani's specialty was healing herbs and potions. There was nothing she enjoyed more than easing the suffering of all living creatures. At the moment most of her patients were animals. Sometimes it seemed as if they were lining up at the cottage door. No matter how wounded, Dani managed to send them away healthier than ever.

One evening, Dani was walking up the steps to the lighthouse, she was met by her little sister, Liza.

"Dani, I looked all over the village for you! Something is wrong with mom. She's in a lot of pain." Dani and Liza ran in the house and up to their mother's room. She was on the bed scrunched into a ball holding her stomach.

"Mom, what's the matter?" Dani asked.

"Nothing, just take care of your sister," she replied in a very weak voice.

Dani and Liza left the room.

"She's been like this a lot during the day but she would usually feel better after a few hours. We went to the village doc a few weeks ago but she said that he told her she was fine. Dani, I'm scared," Liza said.

"Stay with her. I'm gonna get someone. I'll be right back." Dani flew out the door, down the lighthouse steps, running as fast as she could to the cottage. Ingrid opened the door just as Dani was about to grab the knob. Jenna was in bed but jumped up when she heard Dani.

"What is it, Dani?" Jenna asked as she grabbed her robe and sat Dani at the table.

"Something is wrong with my mom! She's really sick," Dani exclaimed as she tried to catch her breath.

"Okay, try to calm down and I will get a few things and we will go to see her," Jenna responded.

Jenna gathered a bunch of herbs, bottles and jars that she thought she may use and she was ready to go. Dani got up and was still trying to catch her breath for the trip back to the lighthouse.

"No time for walking now, Dani," Jenna said and grabbed Dani's hand and pulled her close. Jenna closed her eyes and when she opened them they were at the lighthouse. Dani was about to ask her a thousand questions when Jenna put her finger to Dani's lips and said, "We'll talk about it later. Let's see to your mother."

When they entered the bedroom Dani could see that her mother was in more pain. She looked feverish. Liza was in the chair next to her mother holding her hand. Jenna walked over to the bed and took Gwenevere's other hand. She held it to her chest and closed her eyes. A very faint green light started to surround Gwenevere's hand. Jenna slowly put her hand back down on the bed. She sat silently for a few moments then slowly turned to face Dani. Dani did not like what she saw on Jenna's face.

"Liza, go make us some tea, please," Dani told her sister. "We can heal her, Jenna; you can heal her! What was the point of everything you taught me if we can't heal the first sick person we find? If she can't be healed, then what? Are you telling me she is going to die? I've been spending all my time with you, wasting time, when I should have been here. I could have seen how sick she was. Why didn't I see it? I just wanted to be anywhere but here. Why am I always so selfish? I should have been here! I should have taken care of her instead of some stupid deer!" she yelled at Jenna as the tears rolled down her cheeks and then fell into her arms.

Jenna answered, "Unfortunately, fate has chosen to teach you the hardest lesson of our craft, a lesson that I alone wouldn't have been able to teach you, a lesson that only comes from experience. Sometimes we are all powerless. When it is one's time to leave this world, no matter how much power, money or love you have, nothing can change that. Sometimes all we can do is our best to comfort that soul. If it is her time then there was never anything you could have done. This is not because of anything that you did or didn't do, Dani. However, there is always a chance that I am wrong. I only have a sense about these things, I don't have absolute knowledge when it comes to human health. So let's begin our work. We will throw everything we have at this. We won't give up till it's time to.

Jenna and Dani worked vigorously for three days. They made as many potions as they thought would help. They invoked many healing spells. They meditated for hours trying to draw green healing light to Dani's mother. Even little Liza was helping. She became their assistant running back and forth to the cottage, and with Ingrid's help, would retrieve the things they needed. On the third day Gwenevere awoke in the morning without any pain. She was very weak and was talking softly. Dani was ecstatic. She ran downstairs and started cooking a big breakfast for her mother. Jenna checked on Gwenevere then headed downstairs.

"I knew we could do it! I knew we had the power. We are the most powerful witches that ever existed!" She ran over and hugged Jenna so tightly. When she went to let go Jenna held her tighter.

"Don't do this Dani," whispered Jenna. Dani was struggling now to get away from her. Jenna held her tighter. "We have done our best but it is not over. We have made her comfortable. We have taken away her pain, for now, but she has a long road ahead of her, if she chooses that road." Dani went limp and sobbed in Jenna's arms.

7

There it was! Her father's boat! Finally! Danika ran down the long stretch of stairs from the lighthouse, to the path, to the village. She stood at the dock waiting for the boat to come in. Dani helped her father tie on the boat. Her father jumped down from the ladder and gave her a big, long hug. She was so happy to see his signature smile under his signature mustache. He was a very handsome man who just about matched her mother's beauty. She thought about what a stunning couple they made back in the day as the old pictures and old friends would attest to. As Dani took a better look at her father she became troubled. He didn't look good. He was very thin and a bit hunched over. She told herself that it was because he was at sea and he never takes care of himself when he's on a run. She figured that a few good meals would fill him out. Plus, didn't she have enough on her mind right now. He pulled some salt water taffy out of his pocket and put it in her hand.

"This is all you get today, honey. The haul was shit!" he said. "What's wrong?" he asked when he saw the stress on Dani's face.

"You gotta come to the house, quick," she told him.

When they got to the lighthouse, Liza was showing the village doctor out. She saw her father and flew past the doctor and past Dani and grabbed her father around the waist.

She looked up at him and said "Candy?"

Her father let out a loud laugh then dug in his pocket for the taffy. Liza grabbed a handful then plopped down on the ground and started unwrapping. Dani took her father by the hand and started to lead him over to the doctor who was waiting for them in the doorway.

She yelled back over her shoulder' "Liza! One at a time and only five or I'll kill you."

Dani, her father and the doctor went inside the house.

"Dad, the doc is gonna talk to you about mom. Come up after you're done. Doc, my dad will see you out when you're done filling him in. Thank you for your help," Dani said to the men then walked up the narrow stairs to her mother's bedroom.

A few days later the whole Devlyn family was at the dock. The doctor recommended a hospital across the pond in Boston and wanted Dani"s mother to get there as soon as possible to see a specialist. The boat had been washed down and refueled.

"I don't want to do this," Gwenevere protested. "It's cold, and I hate that boat and it smells like fish and I don't feel sick now, but I will if I get on that smelly boat!"

"But I'll be there to keep you warm," said Errol, and he grabbed his wife and tried to kiss her neck as she tried, without too much effort, to get away from him.

"Like that's gonna make me want to get on that boat!" she said sarcastically.

Liza and Dani watched this scene and rolled their eyes at each other. Liza went a step further and pretended to stick her finger down her throat and gag.

"Gwen, we're just gonna sail down the coast to get to the airport faster so you can get to the hospital. It'll take one day by boat instead of four by car. I promise you'll be comfortable. I fixed the bunk all up for ya. You know you can't waste anymore time. Do it for the girls," Errol pleaded.

"I have a bad feeling about this. But I'm probably gonna drop dead before we get to that hospital anyway," she whispered back to him.

Errol closed his eyes to shake off that remark then, with his big bright, mustached smile, said, "We're off!"

8

Three days later Dani burst into the cottage with Liza in tow.

"Jenna, something is very wrong!" she exclaimed. Jenna ran over to the girls, took them both by the hand and sat them at the table.

"What is it?" she asked as she sat at the small table next to them.

"Mom and dad are missing!" Liza shouted.

"Shut up, Liza!" Dani yelled. Then she explained, "It's been three days since they left. They said they would call when they got to Boston. They should have called last night and they didn't, so I called the hotel and they haven't checked in. I waited a while then called the hospital. Mom's appointment was an hour ago and they never showed up. They never got on the plane or made it to the southern dock. Jenna, they are still at sea!" Jenna could see the panic on Dani's face. Liza was eating a cupcake.

"Did you call the coast guard?' asked Jenna.

"Yes," said Dani, "just before I came here."

"Okay. You and I will go back to the lighthouse and Liza will stay here with Ingrid." said Jenna, calmly taking charge.

"Hooray," yelled Liza, running over to Ingrid and jumping into her lap, squishing the stubborn cat who had been there first.

Danika and Jenna walked to the lighthouse in silence, both trying to analyze the situation. When they got to the door Dani turned to Jenna with a tear streaked face.

She whispered, "I'm scared. I'm scared for them. They are all alone. They are both terrified; I can feel it. Please tell me there is something we can do." Jenna took her gently by the hand and into the house. She brought her over to the fireplace and started a fire. They sat down facing each other. After staring into the fire for a few minutes, Jenna turned back to Dani.

"The only thing I can help you do is to locate them. I can send you to the boat, astrally. Maybe you can help them, I don't know. I don't know what you will find when you get there. If I feel like you are being taken anywhere but the boat, I will have to bring you back immediately; no matter what. The best that will come out of it; maybe you can signal the coast guard or help your father get back on track. You won't have a lot of physical capability, just a little. You can touch and talk but you won't be able to lift or fix anything. The least that will come of it is that you will have closure. Is this what you want to do?"

"I have to. If I don't, I've already begun to fail them," Dani replied.

Jenna took Dani's hands and closed her eyes. Dani did the same. Jenna began.

"Through the veil I send thee, find the trouble on the sea; Through the veil I send thee, find the trouble on the sea; Through the veil I send..."

Dani could smell the salt air and feel the mist touch her skin. She opened her eyes and she was on her father's boat. They were surrounded by the thickest fog. What she could see of the deck looked ransacked. The boat was rocking hard on the waves. She could tell it was adrift. Dani groped along the sides of the boat till she came to the cockpit. She found her father slumped down on the ground. Squatting down next to him she lifted his chin to see if he was alive. At first she couldn't tell but then he opened his eyes.

"Dani," he said in a soft, weak voice, "I can't find your mother. I looked everywhere for her and I couldn't find her. I could hear a whisper of her voice but now I only hear the gulls. They are following me all over the boat. I couldn't stand it anymore so I just hid in here. I'm so cold."

Danika looked at her father's face but could barely recognize him. He was even thinner than before and he looked so old.

"Dad, how did you get lost? Why didn't you may day for help?"

He looked at her and said, "There was a fog. I couldn't see. I tried to find your mother but she won't answer; only the gulls. They try to sneak up on me but I see them out the corner of my eye, the dirty bastards and they run. I tried to steer the boat but my hands don't work. I can't pick anything up. Nothing is working" He held his hands out in front of her and they shook uncontrollably. "I try to walk but my legs keep giving out. I try to tell them to work but they don't listen. Nobody is listening to me." he said as tears started to roll down his face.

Dani held her breath to try to keep herself from crying. She grabbed a thick blanket that was on the floor to drape over him. As she did this she noticed strange symbols, like a sigil, carved in the floor where the blanket had been. She didn't recognize it but knew it did not belong there. She put it in the back of her mind. She needed to help him.

"Daddy, stay here. I'm going to look for mom. Don't move. Everything is going to be okay."

"Do you promise?" he asked.

"Yes" said Dani, and felt a sharp stab of guilt the second she said it because she didn't know if she could help him. She had no Idea what was happening here. It was like a nightmare.

"If you promise, then okay, because I trust you," he replied. Dani already knew his trust was going to haunt her.

Dani went to find her mother. She searched the deck but she wasn't there. Feeling her way around, she found the doorway to the cabin. She went down a few stairs. There were two bunks with a curtain drawn over them. Dani was trembling but knew she had to open that curtain. She pulled it back and her mother lay there, smiling up at her. She looked cold and gray.

"Hello my beautiful girl. I love you so much," she said.

"I Love you too mommy," Dani said as she slid to the floor next to her mother. One of her hands touching the floor felt something peculiar. She looked down and saw the same sigil that was in the cockpit. Again, she could not think about it now but knew it was something out of place; but, then again, is anything really out of place in a nightmare.

"Why didn't you answer daddy when he called?" she asked, turning her attention back to her mother.

"He can't hear me now, sweetheart. He will be able to hear me soon and I will answer him when he calls me."

Dani didn't understand. She thought her mother was delirious. This whole ship seemed to be delirious.

"How is your pain?" Dani asked as she pulled back the covers to check her mother's stomach which is what she would always hold when she was in pain. When Dani saw what was there she fell backwards in horror and hit her head against the wall. Her mother's stomach was hollowed out and in its place were dozens of crabs crawling all around in the empty bowl of her body. Dani, immediately, started to try and get them off but her mother grabbed her hand and stopped her.

"They have already taken me, Dani. But it's okay. I'm used to them now and it doesn't hurt anymore because they are done eating. I know each and every one of them. Each one is a worry I had, or a fear, or an anxiety or pain. They just became hungry for more and, I guess, even with all my pain and worry that I've had in my life, they still couldn't get enough. So here they are. I'm so sorry. I didn't want you to see this, and I don't know what to do about your father. I'm sure you will figure something out." Gwenevere's voice became very faint and she stopped speaking for a moment. She seemed to be listening to something but then she continued.

"I'm going now, to be with my mother. I've missed her so much. Promise me something?"

Oh no, Dani thought, not another promise.

"Anything mommy," she heard herself say.

"Take care of your sister and don't cry. Don't be sad. All I've ever wanted my whole life was for my girls to be happy. Tell Liza how much I love her. I love you."

With that Gwenevere turned lighter and lighter gray; then turned to ash. The ash blew away with the wind that streamed through the cabin and the crabs scurried away to a hole in the boat and escaped out to sea to find a new carcass to fester in.

Dani could feel Jenna want to pull her back.

She told her, "Not yet!"

She jumped up and ran back to the cockpit to find her father. Dani was terrified and couldn't understand why this was happening. Her father was not where she had left him. She went out onto the deck, into the dense fog. She heard her father sobbing. He had managed to get one leg up and was sliding himself over the side of the boat. When she spotted him she stopped in her tracks.

"Dad, what are you doing?" she yelled in a panic.

"Can't steer my boat. I can't control anything on my boat. What kind of captain am I if I can't control my own boat? I lost my wife. I don't know where she is. I'm lost without her. I'm going to find her. I think she's down there" he said pointing with his trembling hand. He disappeared over the side of the boat and Dani leaped in after him; into the freezing ocean. She grabbed his hand but had no power to pull him up. Instead, he was pulling her down, deeper and deeper into the darkness.

"I love you daddy," she yelled to him, knowing that she had to let go or be dragged down with him.

"Am I dying?" he called to her as he suddenly realized what was happening to him.

"I think so daddy," Dani choked out the response, "I'm sorry! I thought I could save you! I tried. I can't do it. I don't have the strength!"

With that, Dani let go of her father's hand and she watched his face fade into the darkness. Jenna pulled Dani up through the water and through the veil. They sat in front of the fireplace holding each other, sobbing, in a puddle of cold sea water.

9

That night Dani came down with a fever. She was in bed for weeks. Jenna and Ingrid were by her side day and night using every bit of healing power that they could. Jenna was terrified. One night she cried in Ingrid's lap while she stroked Jenna's hair, trying her best to comfort her.

"What is happening to her? Why won't she get better? If I lose her, I think I will die!" Jenna cried.

"You have answered your own question, little one. If we all choose to die when a loved one dies, we would all be gone from this world." she answered with her deep voice and Slavic accent. "This is what she is feeling, no? She has lost her will because she has lost her parents. It is a terrible thing she has gone through. She feels responsible because she could not save them. You told her that what is, must be. But she is choosing to ignore your wisdom. It was their time. Even though I think something else may have been responsible."

"What do you mean?" Jenna jumped up and swiped away her tears, ashamed of herself for breaking down in the first place.

"The sigils," Ingrid answered, "From what you described, those sigils that were carved into the boat are black magic, I'm sure of it."

"Why would anyone want to hurt those poor people?" asked Jenna.

"Not Danika's parents; Danika. This was done to harm her, to weaken her so she does not reach her full potential. They have done a good job, as well. She doesn't have the will to live, nevermind to reach her full power."

"I will destroy whoever has done this!" Jenna proclaimed, feeling rage welling up inside her replacing the sadness she was full of a moment ago.

Ingrid grabbed her by the arm as she was ready to storm out in search of revenge. Igrid felt a shock of electricity when she did this. Jenna's rage was filling her power.

"Stop!" Ingrid told her. "Use your head, girl! If this is enraging you think how Dani will feel when you tell her. This will get her out of that bed in a heartbeat."

Jenna stopped and slowly turned back around and listened as Ingrid continued.

"Neither sickness, nor sadness will have a place in that body once she hears of this. But, mark my words, you must plan before you tell her. You must have a path set for her to get her revenge or she will go off the rails.

"Do not misunderstand, I condone no black magic. I just want her out of that bed. Also, I want her protected from whoever would dare to harm any of us. That is the only reason I am telling you any of this. Her revenge should be, to become who she was meant to be. Whoever did this went to great lengths to try and stop that. We will give her another month to get herself together then we will have her initiation and her transference to the Archive." Ingrid stopped talking and looked to see if Jenna completely grasped the meaning of this statement.

Jenna was following everything Ingrid was saying and was realizing why this witch was revered. She had the wisdom of a sage. This would get Dani up and out of her depression. Jenna knew that Dani would want to do anything she could to avenge her parents, once she knew there was foul play involved. All this will fuel her power and will electrify her initiation. Wait till Dani finds out she is to be initiated, Jenna thought; and to become the Archive...to be Archive. The full meaning finally hit her.

" Ingrid, no! You will die!" Jenna cried.

"What do you think we've been doing with this child! Why do you think you found her? This is her destiny and it will be fulfilled! The timing is perfect," Ingrid yelled back at her.

"I don't want you to go," Jenna said as she slid to the floor and put her head back in Ingrid's lap.

Ingrid stroked her hair again then kissed her head.

"I know this will be hard for you, my darling. You are the strongest and most cunning of the coven and this is why you lead them. I am so proud of you. We will both be proud of her. Her time is now. My time to move on is now. I am so tired, Jenna. I have been here a very, very long time. Even though I was chosen to be the Archive, almost three hundred years ago, for my endurance, one can only endure so long. It is my time to return to the source for my eternal peace.

"I feel like you are making me choose between you and Dani," Jenna whispered.

"Nonsense," Ingrid replied, " the choice was made the day she found you. Have a clear conscience, my dear, this was never your choice to make. Besides, I will always be with you. You know this."

Jenna and Ingrid stayed this way for a while. Jenna absorbed all this information into her mind while Ingrid stroked her hair. She knew she was right about everything and was surprised at herself for having such a selfish reaction. Jenna sat up, stretched and yawned.

"I will sleep on this and have the perfect plan of attack by morning. Then I will raise our 'Lazarus' from her grave and start a fire under her that will take a typhoon to quench!"

"That's the spirit!" Ingrid clapped her hands together and leaned back in her rocking chair.

10

"The sigils!" Dani exclaimed. I can barely remember them now. I knew there was something wrong with them being there. How do you know for sure that they were a curse?"

"That night you described them to me perfectly and I drew them on paper. The next day, while you slept, I showed Ingrid. She saw them for what they were; a curse, and a strong one at that," Jenna explained.

"But why, Jenna, why? I'm no threat to anyone. What kind of evil creature kills someone's parents just to weaken their spirit?" At this point Dani was feeling a powerful mix of sadness and anger. Jenna brought Dani over to the large oak tree in the front yard. She was still weak so Jenna held onto her as they walked. Jenna sat her down on a blanket in the grass.

"I am going to explain some things to you Dani and I need you to understand the gravity of what I am about to tell you. When we first met I told you that I would ask something of you in return for my training. Do you remember Dani?"

"Yes, I do. I would do anything for you, you know that," Dani answered.

"What I am asking of you now isn't just for me but for all beings that use the powers provided by the earth, the air, the fire, the water and the spirit. You will be initiated during this coming Solstice. Directly after that ceremony there will be another. You will take Ingrid's place as the Archive." Jenna stared at Dani, intently, holding her breath in anticipation of what she was about to explain to her.

"What is an Archive?" Dani asked, and Jenna released her breath to answer.

"The Archive is a powerful witch who has great endurance and strength. She carries the knowledge of all our craft for three hundred years, at which time she will transfer to the next chosen initiate and be released."

"Why does this sound like a very long prison sentence?" Dani asked.

"It is not a sentence when given to one who can endure. When I say endure, I mean being alive for three hundred years. You cannot die or be killed. Imagine what you can achieve with that time; what experiences you can have. All Archives have been incredibly important beings in this world, in addition to storing the secrets, and you will too. This has gone on since the beginning of the time of men and creatures.

"The downside is, that, along with the joys of many many lifetimes you will experience, you will also experience many losses. What regular people experience in death and loss of the ones they love, you will have three fold. This is exceptionally painful should you find your soul mate. You will have to go three lifetimes before you can meet them again." Jenna took another deep breath. She had not realized how difficult it would be to explain this to Dani. She also had not realized the depth of sacrifice this title inflicted on its chosen vessels. Until now she had mostly focused on the glory of carrying the knowledge, of the power and longevity to accomplish three times more than anyone else. She now thought of Ingrid and what she must have been through over these many, many years. Now she understood why Ingrid was ready to move on.

"Jenna," Dani said looking very seriously at her, "I highly recommend that you never go into sales."

They burst out laughing, then sat quietly for a few moments, both processing their thoughts.

Dani squeezed Jenna's hands then said, "I will do anything you ask of me, you should know this. I assume Ingrid isn't explaining this to me herself because it would exhaust her; it's exhausted you and you're not even 'the chosen'. But if she did explain it to me I'm sure she would tell me that I will learn as I go. She says that to me about everything. Besides, it must not be too terrible of a job seeing that it has been done since the beginning of time. As long as you are with me for as long as I can have you, then I'm good."

"You never cease to amaze me Danika. You have wisdom beyond your years. I can see why you were chosen. I always have," There was silence once again as Jenna gathered the courage to tell Dani the last part of what the transfer entailed.

"Dani, Ingrid, is exhausted. She has served us all with her strength and endurance and because of her, ancient knowledge will once again be passed on to generations of witches. When she transfers the sacred knowledge to you, Dani, she will leave this world. She will return to the source for eternal peace. This is what must be." She watched Dani absorb the magnitude of what she was just told. Dani was quiet for a few minutes.

"Is this the way it has always been done?" she asked.

"Yes", Jenna replied.

"She has talked to you about this and this is what she wants?" Dani asked.

47

"Yes. She is ready. We will be pained not to have her in our lives anymore but we must respect her decision. You also need to know that you are making this transition even more joyful for her because she is so proud to have you as her successor. She has nothing but faith in you as the next Archive."

"I will not disappoint her. My own mother told me not to cry for her and I will not cause Ingrid pain by crying for her, either. I will be strong for her, for us," Dani said with a mixed feeling of conviction and sadness.

"Ingrid will be pleased when I tell her," said Jenna.

Dani collected her thoughts for a moment.

"What happened to my parents, was it because I am to be the Archive?" she asked.

"We believe so," Jenna responded.

"How would killing my family benefit anyone?"

"They probably wanted you in a mentally and physically weakened state so the transfer would be weak. They, then, could try to obtain the sacred knowledge from you or Ingrid as you would both be weak and vulnerable."

"Who?" asked Dani, "Who has that kind of power?"

"The Coven of Darkness, Dani, that's who. Remember our friend , Magda? She's one of their bulldogs. They are a nasty bit of work. Their main goal is to bring fear back to the world. They believe that people have no beliefs anymore, especially in the gods. They think people only fear the pain that they inflict on each other; which to me is horrific enough. They want to possess the knowledge then raise the lesser gods; the malevolent ones. With that, they believe, humans will have to look to them for the protection they once needed or ways to appease the gods and be protected from these forces. They think this will exalt them to power over the world. This is an abridged version of the nonsense that floats around during their Sabbaths. But you know how it goes, get enough crazy together and bad things happen every time."

"Well, they have messed with the wrong witch. All hell is not going to be breaking loose on my watch! Let's go tell Ingrid the good news and let's enjoy her company while we still have her. I hope she made something really good for dinner, I'm starving. I guess making plans for the next three hundred years can do that to a girl," Dani stated as she pulled Jenna off the ground. Jenna was very happy to see that Ingrid's advice paid off. Dani's strength was coming back. Her healing would be fast now.

11

A month later Danika was primed and ready. She felt better than she had ever felt. Emotionally, she had steadied herself through sheer will. As Jenna told her, the only way to avenge her parents was to reach her full power; to become everything she was put on this earth to be and she planned on making that happen. Physically, she had never felt better. She was healthy and full of life and youth; a maiden in the awakening of desire, feeling a lust for life and everything it had to offer her. Tonight's special Sabbath during the Summer Solstice would be her initiation into the coven. She would become one with her sisters and with the earth that they worshiped; the earth that was the source of their powers.

Preparations had been made for this evening's ceremony. The other witches were traveling in from other parts of the countryside. Jenna had arranged for one of the elders who would not be participating in the ceremonies to stay with little Liza. Dani had been fasting for three days. When she woke that morning she was feeling light headed which added to the hefty feel of magic that was in the air. Despite a little weakness, Dani was eager for things to start. It was almost like all the cells of her body were yearning to connect to something that was just about in reach. Jenna did not give too much instruction other than the fast. She said that Dani would be led to the forest where the ceremony would begin and she should just do what she felt she should. The sisters would guide her and be there to support her.

The sun began to set. The thirteen witches assembled at the edge of the forest wearing white gowns. They anointed each other with sacred oils on the forehead to open their senses. Jenna adorned Dani with a wreath of cedar and elder twigs to connect to the power of the forest and the summer solstice. Each of them lit a single white candle then began the procession down the forest path. They came to a clearing that was lit by the moon like a spotlight. A pyre had been assembled earlier that day. The women circled around the pyre and each one stuck their candle into the ground in front of them. Jenna raised her arms and the pyre was lit. Simultaneously they let their gowns fall to the ground. They began to sway back and forth letting their bodies loose. They began to hum and moan and breathe deeply, in and out. The humming and droning became louder and louder and their movements more intense. When the many movements and different sounds grew into one, Jenna fell to the ground on her hands and knees; the others did the same. Only Jenna arose. She summoned Danika who walked around from the opposite side of the fire and stood before her. Jenna picked up a small copper bowl that contained paint conjured from an ancient potion and she used her finger to paint offering symbols on Dani's forehead, chest, breasts and abdomen. She had Dani drink, fully, from a silver goblet containing an elixir made from the blackened hoof mushrooms. This elixir would open Dani's mind and all her senses, fully, so she could see all the forces of nature that existed in the forest. Jenna then turned Dani around to face her sisters.

"Here stands before this sacred coven, a bud that has grown from the roots of land. We have nurtured her in the sacred arts and she has excelled in our practices. Let her now go into the forest to become one with it; to offer the forest her maidenhood which will be the key to opening its treasures to her, forever. So mote it be."

"So mote it be," the coven said back in unison.

Jenna stepped aside and turned Dani toward the continuing path. The women began to chant sacred words and sway and move again. Dani walked on into the thickest canopy of trees and could hear the fervent hum of the coven getting lost behind her. She walked on feeling as though she were in a dream, barely feeling the ground beneath her. She finally came to a lush patch of the softest grass she had ever felt. In front of her was a strong and mighty oak tree. Beyond that was a small waterfall that sent down a gentle stream of water that glistened in what moonlight could break through the thick canopy. Fireflies darted around and frogs playfully hopped back and forth. Dani felt sleepy and languidly laid down on the blanket of grass beneath the tree, staring up at it while she touched the trunk of it, playfully, with her toes. She listened to all the sounds of the forest mixed with the chanting of the coven in the distance. The grass beneath her was like a cloud and the twinkling moonlight was mesmerizing. Her body began to react strongly to the rich stimuli that surrounded her. Every piece of her skin craved to be caressed. No sooner did she have that thought, then arms of the lush grass wrapped themselves around her. The arms had strong hands that caressed her with the silky softness of the grass. She could feel the grass beneath her become warm and legs of grass welled up from the ground next to her legs. She was cradled now in a strong body beneath her and her body writhed against it. The hands enveloped her breast and squeezed them and circled them. A leg slid under her and in between her legs and she grinded against it. A hand moved up and grabbed her by her throat and jaw and she could feel another's face pressed against the side of her own. The other hand of the body that rose beneath her dove in between her legs and rubbed and squeezed and penetrated her to the point of ecstasy. Dani started to sense what was happening and turned atop the creature under her. She was straddling a man; but not a man. He was the forest. He was the Green Man. She reached out and caressed his face which had a beard and hair of leaves that were the most glorious shades of green she had ever seen. His eyes were mysterious and deep brown, like the richest soil, beneath his strong brow and they glowed in the moonlight. His body was magnificent with the muscles of the finest specimen of a man yet it was of the forest and covered with leaves and bark instead of hair and skin. He smiled at her as she studied his appearance without the slightest sign of fear or hesitation, only admiration and desire. He spoke softly to her.

"You are doing well my child. I am happy that you are enjoying our consummation. I knew you would. You are one of my kind. I have been eager for your initiation since you came of age. I have watched you since you stepped foot in me when you were a tiny girl chasing dragonflies and climbing my trees. You have loved me the day you discovered me and I've known this. I've been waiting patiently to love you back, Danika. I will enter you now as you entered me those many years ago. We will become one and I will fill you my secrets with you. The living things that live and grow in me will be at your call. You will have the power to heal and the power to harm. Your nature, which is of kindness, will guide you well to deal out those services as you see fit. There are not many who love me as you do and it thrills me to give you my gifts.

The Green Man rose from the ground holding Dani in his arms as he did. He put her down in front of him and stood before her, seven feet tall; a man, a creature, a god, the forest itself. His smooth branch was fully erect and Dani could not help herself but to reach out and caress him as she would have had she been exploring the forest and found a forbidden fruit. He reached out and ran his fingers through her hair then lifted her up and placed her on her back where the soft grass had been refilled. She opened her legs for him and he knelt down in front of her and leaned over her, entering her, filling her. She pulled him into her, deeper still and they stayed that way looking into each other's eyes almost challenging each other to move. Then they did move, wildly, thrusting in and pulling out of each. Dani met the mighty creatures every move. He penetrated her over and over, deeper and deeper until the dam could no longer hold. The Green Man came into her, filling her vessel with the seeds of all the knowledge that his domain could give her and she absorbed it with wave after wave of pleasure.

Dani was awakened by her hair being pulled. She was naked, lying on her belly in the plush grass and a hare was taking a nibble on her hair.

"Stop that," she whispered firmly, then gently pushed the rabbit away by his nose. She remembered where she was and ran her hands up and down the soft grass then kissed the ground beneath her.

"Thank you for a beautiful evening that I will never forget," she said, then began to rise. She was cold and had no idea how long she had been there. She could still feel the pulsating between her legs as she walked back down the path where she could see the light of the coven's fire.

When she got back to the clearing the witches were sitting still as statues around the fire. Jenna got up and walked Dani back over to the circle. The other witches stood up. Jenna raised Dani's hand.

"Sisters, a child entered the forest and has returned a maiden and now, the thirteenth member of this coven. We give thanks to the Green Man for accepting our offering and for returning the maiden with the sacred knowledge that binds this coven to each other and to the earth. So mote it be"

"So mote it be," responded the coven.

"Circle the fire Danika and you will join your sisters in flight," Jenna said as she pushed Dani away. Dani ran around the fire as the witches watched from the shadows and whispered, "Rise, rise, rise." Dani felt the heat from the fire and reveled in it. She ran faster and faster and they chanted louder now, "Rise, rise, rise, rise." Looking up at the black sky darted with crystal stars, Dani began to feel that feeling in the top of her stomach just below her heart and she let out the laughter of a mad woman, then she rose. She floated above the ground still circling the fire with her hair, her legs, her arms flowing weightlessly behind her. As she ascended higher she looked down and saw the others starting to rise, one after another. They all howled with laughter and delight as they filled the night sky with their naked bodies and their wild abandon.

Once again, Dani was awakened, but this time by Jenna who was beckoning her to come with her. Dani saw that she and her sisters were all sleeping in a circle around the fire, which was now very dim.

"Your night is not over, my sweet. There is one more task for you to fulfill," Jenna whispered to her.

She took Dani by the hand and they walked in a new direction through the forest. Dani felt the forest in a whole new way now; as if it were an extension of herself. Her feet did not seem to separate from the ground as she walked. She felt as though there were invisible fibers in the space between her foot and the ground. Not too far off, they came upon a cave. Dani could see fire light dancing on the inside of the cave wall. Jenna led her in.

The cave was filled with the heavy scent of incense. Dani could sense the spirits of many witches in this place. There was a sacredness here that she had never felt before. When her eyes adjusted better, Dani noticed a woman sitting on the ground atop some woven blankets and wearing one around her shoulders. Jenna gently nudged Dani forward then bowed reverently and left the cave. Dani began to shiver despite the fire.

"Come to me , my child," said a husky voice with a Slavic accent.

Dani realized the woman was Ingrid. She had forgotten her last task in the frenzy of the night's events. This, she could tell, was going to be a much different experience. Ingrid took Dani's hand and pulled her down to her. She put her blanket around Dani and cradled her in her lap. She looked down at Dani and into her eyes. Ingrid's face was radiant. She gently kissed Dani's forehead and stroked her hair.

"My precious child, you have made us so proud. You are at the very precipice of your very long life. Being charged with the honor of Archive, you will not die until you pass the knowledge in this way to another as worthy as yourself, three hundred years from now. You have been chosen for your strength and endurance. You will live a rich and fulfilling life. You shall ease the suffering of many. I see your soulmate in this lifetime. Your mate's soul will seem damaged beyond repair and will be your greatest healing challenge. Once this soul is healed you will have a fierce protector which you will need in the years to come. Be sure, my child, your road is as long and hard as it will be glorious.

"You will now receive the sacred knowledge of our craft from the beginning of time. I charge you to become the Archive as I transfer my power and knowledge to you. This is an honor and responsibility granted to very few witches and I grant it to you now."

Ingrid lowered the blanket from her shoulder and exposed her breast. She put her nipple to Dani's lips. Dani tasted warm, sweet milk as it began to flow into her mouth. She drank. She consumed the sacred knowledge as it poured into her. Her mind began to explode with images from the beginning of time. The more she drank the more and more alive she felt. She could feel the light of the sun shining through her and overtaking the darkness of the cave until there was nothing but light. Then she felt Ingrid's soul pass through her like ice water; not unpleasant, but refreshing, exhilarating. Dani's mouth let go of the breast and she gasped for air. When she opened her eyes she looked up at Ingrid who still held her so motherly. She was gone. Dani sat up and pulled Ingrid's body into her arms and cradled her now. She pulled the covers around them both and fell asleep by the fire.

The next morning the members of the coven all gathered at the cave in silence. Danika came to the mouth of the cave where Jenna met her and put a warm black cloak around her. They entered the cave and four of the sisters laid Ingrid's body on a soft blanket then prepared it for burial. When they were finished they covered her with a shroud of elaborate design. The rest of the sisters all surrounded the blanket then each picked up some of it and lifted her. Jenna lifted a torch and led a procession deep into the cave to an alcove that had been prepared to house Ingrid's body in the company of all past Archives. When her body was placed in the alcove, whispers of welcome could be heard echoing throughout the cave. A large stone was rolled in front to seal the remains. Dani and Jenna were the last to leave the cave.

12

Over the next five years, Danika practiced intense magic. Having the knowledge stored inside her made her very powerful. It took very little effort for her to conjure or enchant. Her spells were extraordinary. Jenna's biggest challenge was teaching Dani restraint. She had to remind her over and over that the use of magic came with a price; that there must always be balance and sacrifice for what was given by the spirit and by the earth. The forest was their territory and it shared with their coven graciously, but Dani began to venture out to new places. She spent a lot of time at the beach and in the ocean. When she put her bare feet on the sand she felt strong energy flow through her. When she swam in the ocean she could feel the animals that swam near her. Sometimes she would float face down as long as she could and when she did this, she could feel herself become one with the ocean and she could feel the shores of the lands it connected to. The salt water was an incredible conduit for her and she, for it. She practiced this over and over for longer and longer amounts of time. The longer she stayed under the further she could go into different lands, connecting to its earth. She told Jenna that it was like introducing herself to these new places and they were all welcoming her. She knew that she would have access to all the earth like she had to their forest. Her power had become vast. She was starting to become restless and wanted to explore new places.

Dani was also becoming an accomplished artist. She painted scenes of her ocean and her forest and of the small village near the lighthouse. Painting was a perfect form of meditation for her. Hours would pass like minutes and she would have exquisite paintings done, but feel as though she had just started. Painting connected her to herself, to her human talent. When Dani painted she used no witchcraft, only her love of the feel of the paint sliding against the canvas or the brush wafting through the beautiful colors of paint. It reminded her of herself before the craft or the knowledge, when her mind and hands created their own magic from within herself; a human magic. Her love of the forest and the ocean and all the creatures inspired her everyday, just as they inspired her when she was a child. She could see the circle of her life in her love of painting and of the ocean and forest and her craft. It was all connected. It was all magical.

Dani would bring her paintings to a small gallery in Boscastle. It was a touristy area and the paintings sold very well, to the point that she had built a nice little nest egg. That day Dani had driven her parent's old car to the town to deliver some of her paintings. It was a bit far, but she liked the solitude to think for a while and the change of scenery helped get her mind energized. Her thoughts were of her parents and how she couldn't believe that so much time had passed since they were taken from her and her sister. The thought of sadness always turned to anger when she remembered that her parents were deliberately taken from her. Sometimes she would start to wonder if Ingrid was right about the coven of Darkness being responsible because nothing else had happened over the last five years. But, then she would remember the nightmare she witnessed on that boat and knew in her heart that something truly evil had to be responsible for what happened. It was just very strange how life has just gone on after such a horrible experience and without her parents, who she loved dearly and missed so much.

She also thought how proud she was of Liza, who was now fifteen. This would bring Dani out of her negative spiral. Liza was staying with Jenna at the cottage; it made her too sad to be at the lighthouse. Jenna was seeing to her training in the craft. Liza was very smart, sometimes too much for her own good. She would get bored very easily and Jenna finally caught on that she needed to be constantly challenged or Liza would be challenging. Jenna did not like having to be a child psychologist but did her best because she knew Liza had a gift; they just couldn't put their finger on what it was. Luckily, for Jenna, a distraction had arrived at the cottage in the form of one of the coven sisters who was having a terrible time with ghosts.

One night Dani Jenna and Liza were relaxing after a long day of work when a frantic knock on the door made them all jump. Two of the coven sisters were carrying a third, who was holding her head in anguish. The two explained that this witch was an exemplary medium who has helped many people connect to loved ones who had passed on and helped spirits give messages to the living. The problem was that the spirits have become a severe nuisance and they were calling to her constantly, to the point that she could barely have any of her own thoughts. She felt as if her head would explode and couldn't bear it any longer. The two witches had brought Anne Marie to the cottage in hopes that Dani and Jenna could help her. They agreed and got to work that night. Because Anne Marie was a medium they couldn't make the spirits go away as they were naturally drawn to her. They needed a way to make them get in line and not try to get to her all at once. Jenna came up with the idea of making a door that the spirits would need to wait at. Anne Marie would have to open and give the ghost permission to come through. With Dani and Jenna's help they were able to install the door in Anne Marie's mind and the chaos stopped. After a few days the pain in her head had gone away and Anne Marie was able to control the spirits perfectly. They all agreed that she should stay awhile to make sure the door held. Being an extremely loving and motherly person, Anne Marie took right to Liza and became a great asset to Liza and Jenna. She had remained there ever since filling the void that Ingrid's absence had created. Life certainly did go on, Dani thought, and we learn something new everyday. Who would have thought that ghosts could be a cause for migraines!

She arrived at the gallery and laughed to herself about how she had been so wrapped up in her rambling thoughts that it didn't even seem like she was in a car driving down long bumpy roads. Dani went to the boot of the car, opened it and took out a bunch of finished paintings. She crossed the street and walked to the gallery. The director of the gallery was delighted with the new paintings and gave Dani her commission on the last ones that she had dropped off. It was their busy season and she was doing really well. Dani thanked the director and was on her way.

As Dani exited the gallery she felt the adrenaline of danger rush through her body. She looked around to see what was coming. There was nothing. Dani did not move, she just waited and observed her surroundings like Jenna had taught her. She then heard a loud screech. A little girl had ridden her bike across the street and a car jammed on its brakes to stop from hitting her. Dani could see that there was a car coming right behind the one that stopped and was about to push it right into the girl who was standing, frozen, in front of the stopped car. Danika raised her hand in front of her and called as much force as she could collect in a second then sent it toward the little girl and pushed her out of the way. The oncoming car collided with the stopped car and sent it flying. Crash, crash, crash! Dani ran across the street, looked into the cars and saw that the passengers were okay then ran to the girl. Dani scooped her up in her arms and held her until her mother came running over and grabbed her.

"Thank you! I don't know what happened, I was right behind her and looked down for a second. When I looked up there was nothing but crashing. Thank God she's okay!" the mother said as she cried.

"Here comes an ambulance, someone must have called. Bring her to them and have them check her over, but I think she is just fine," she told the woman.

Dani stuck around in the back of a crowd watching the commotion. All of a sudden she experienced another rush of danger but this time she wasn't fast enough. A person who had walked up next to her blew a powder in her face and she passed out immediately. Two others caught her and pulled her into a car. No one saw a thing as they were too busy watching the drivers of the cars yelling at each other.

13

Danika woke up chained by her wrists and ankles to a wall inside a cave. She felt like her head had been smashed in and she was very dizzy and disoriented. She could see a fire about twenty feet away from her and there were three cloaked figures sitting around it, chanting. There was a suffocating feel of magic in this place. Dani felt as though she could barely breathe. Just opening her eyes was taking all the effort she had. Someone had been standing next to her in the shadows and when they saw her eyes were open they sounded an alarm. A cloaked figure appeared before Dani and blew the powder in her face again rendering her unconscious.

"That was close," said one of the cloaked figures, "I can not believe that she could wake from the paralyzer, but you were right Magda. This one's strength is extraordinary."

"Yes and, unfortunately for us, it makes it harder to break into her. We don't have the pleasure of time which is what it will take to drill a hole through her shield and into the Archive. Then, after that difficult work we must begin the extraction. If we can keep her frozen long enough, before her mind finds a way to unparalyze, then we can make this happen. Get a new trio to pray at the sacred fire. We will need another sacrifice for the Dark One, soon. We must maintain the pressure of all our powers to break her. Go now," commanded Magda, the newly anointed priestess of the coven of Darkness.

Magda had waited most patiently to come into her power and her main objective was to obtain the knowledge of the Archive. The last priestess out right refused to steal the knowledge even though it was a primary directive in their plans to gain power over all the earth; its humans, beast, elements, everything. That weak priestess still feared retribution of balance and obviously did not have enough faith in the Darkness to hold them above all once the knowledge was theirs. Magda had been groomed by the Darkness since she was a child and was now ready to challenge this new powerful Archive. From what she saw of her the day they met in the dark forest, Magda had not been impressed. Even with the challenge this witch was presenting at the moment she was not daunted and could feel victory in her grasp. She could feel the Darkness rising up to take its place over the earth, with her at its side. The thought excited her to action and she joined the new group of witches at the fire and lent her own power to the intention of breaking Danika's shield.

14

"Can't anyone answer the door?" shouted Anne Marie. Jenna and Dani looked up at her in shock. They had never heard her yell before. Anne Marie was the most soft spoken, agreeable lady they had ever met.

" Anne Marie, no one is knocking on the door," Liza told her.

" Fine," said Anne Marie in a huff. She threw down the dough she had been kneading, wiped the flower on her apron then stormed over to the door and threw it open. There was no one there. She looked all around the front yard then came back in and slowly closed the door behind her.

"I'm sorry. I must have been day dreaming, but it sounded so real." She started to walk back to the kitchen counter but grabbed her head and fell to the ground. Jenna and Liza ran over to her.

"What is happening," Jenna asked, trying to get Anne Marie to focus on her.

"The knocking! It is so loud. It's a spirit. They won't stop pounding on the door. I'm afraid to open it. What if it's all of them and they all rush through? Jenna, what do I do?" She asked frantically.

"Open it," Jenna told her, "we are with you. We will protect you. See what this intrusion is. It is most unusual."

Anne Marie opened the door in her mind and Gwenever walked through.

"My daughter is in grave danger. You must tell Jenna that Danika is in the Dark forest. They are trying to steal the Archive. Help her and she can then avenge my death," said the spirit in desperation then faded from Anne Marie's consciousness. Anne Marie told Jenna and Liza what Gwenevere had said. Liza burst into tears, upset that she didn't get to speak to her mother. Jenna was incredulous.

"How was she taken without me knowing? I would have felt something. Are you sure it was Gwenevere and not some trouble making ghost?" Jenna asked.

"No, it was her and she was as panicked as you are now. Go Jenna! You have to help her. I will take care of Liza. And you, Liza, stop crying! Your mother loves you so much. She will be back to talk to you soon. Today she was an omen, there was no time for pleasure," Anne Marie said as she grabbed Liza and hugged her like only a mother could. Liza calmed down immediately.

Jenna was out the door and saddling Mystery. She rode hard till the mist appeared. Mystery jumped through and galloped fast as her mighty legs would go. She jumped through to the other side and reared up on her hind quarters in fright for before them was part of the Coven of Darkness who had been waiting for them to arrive. Jenna was thrown off of Mystery and when she got her bearings and tried to get up one of the coven blew the paralyzing powder into her face and she was out.

"Bind her, leave the horse," said the leader and they were off.

15

"Wake up!" Magda said as she happily slapped Danika's face. Dani opened her eyes and found Magda squatting down in front of her holding her up by the collar of her shirt.

"Mother may I?" Dani said coyly as she tried to struggle free from Magda's grip. " This is going to go very poorly for you Magda. You really should have tried this a long time ago instead of letting me hone my powers. I hope you have a pretty good plan."

"Oh I do, Danika," she said as she stepped aside and revealed Jenna's naked body tied to a ceremonial altar and all the coven of Darkness standing around it waiting for the head to arrive.

"You will give me what I want or she is our next sacrifice and our Master has been waiting to sink his teeth into her for years. To be honest I really don't think he intends to let either one of you out of here alive, but, if you cooperate I can see to it myself. I am going to the head of that altar to start the summoning. If I sense your shield coming down then I will stop, otherwise he will arrive and gorge himself with her body."

Magda dropped Dani, turned and walked over to the altar. She took her position and started the summoning.

"Oh Dark One, we, your disciples, wake you to do you homage and give you a powerful gift to momentarily quell your never ending hunger; a hunger only the darkening of the world will fill. Come to us and grace us with your malice and rage as we may pass on that malice and rage to all beings in this lowly world that seek to keep you in the underworld. So mote it be."

"So mote it be," responded the coven.

Magda raised the sacred chalice in one hand and the athame in the other. She raised Jenna's arm and cut it with the athame and collected the blood in the chalice and she drank. Danika felt an enormous swell of rage as she watched Jenna's blood drip down the sides of Magda's lips. She could barely think straight after all the potions Magda had put in her and she was still extremely weak but she was feeling terrified at the idea of Jenna being hurt.

All of a sudden the light in the cave went very dim and it seemed as though the air was being sucked out of it. A horrible smell wafted through the cave. The ground began to shake. At the foot of the altar, now stood a tall man dressed all in white with platinum blonde hair and the palest blue eyes. He was not at all what one might picture a god called the Dark One to look like.

"My children, you have all done well. I feel the powerful sacrifice you have brought me. You are too kind." Danika strained to hear him as he spoke almost in a whisper. The Dark One walked around the altar and touched each member of the coven then walked back to Magda.

"My Lord, we are honored by your presence and offer you the gift of the high priestess of the Green Forest coven. Feast on her power and her being and grant us your blessing," and with that Magda bowed her head and stepped aside so her master could take Jenna. At this moment Jenna came to, to see the pale blue eyes of destruction looking down at her and she screamed in terror.

"Stop!" Danika screamed, and for a second the Dark One was frozen then began to slowly turn his head in Dani's direction.

"I thought the power was much, too much to be coming from the little bird on the table. My priestess, is there something you would like to explain to me?" he asked Magda as he stared ravenously at Dani.

"My Lord, she is the Archive. With your power we shall drain her of the knowledge and plunge the world into darkness and all will be your subjects."

"My priestess, do you mean to dictate to me?" the Dark One asked, ominously.

"No my Lord," Magda responded, not so confident now.

"No indeed. Who decided that I need to rule anywhere but my little section of the underworld. I am quite comfortable torturing the souls of the damned. In this world they create themselves everyday. I have new toys to play with whenever I want them. If I came here, how would new souls be born with the free will which they then choose to squander. The souls are much more delicious when they choose to come to me. No, I think I will remain where I am. I will accept this sacrifice, she is terribly irresistible. Her suffering will be delectable."

"You must give me the knowledge of the Archive! I demand it. We have worshiped you and done your bidding; everything you have asked!" Magda yelled in an almost crazed state.

"You dare make a demand of me? That's a first, congratulations. You have outdone yourself with pride. Too bad you are the most delusional witch I have ever met. You could have been dangerous if you weren't just deranged," and with that Magda's head draped over the side of her broken neck, eyes wide with rage. The other members of the coven began to scream in agony as their bones were broken in hundreds of pieces until there were no more bones left to break. Then, silence.

The Dark One looked down at Jenna and opened his mouth until his jaw unhinged and rows of shards of teeth protruded and saliva of the foulest stench dripped off of them. All Jenna could do was scream.

Jenna's scream sent all of Dani's rage to the forefront of her being until the parameter of her body could not contain it. A destructive force shot out of her straight at the Dark One and obliterated him. He covered the entire cave with the entrails and gore and blood of his human form. Dani, now free from her chains, ran over to Jenna and untied her from the altar.

"You killed him, Danika. He is completely gone. Not just the body but his spirit as well. I can't sense it anywhere. No one can kill a god, Danika, it is not possible," Jenna said in disbelief of what she just witnessed.

"Yeah? Tell him that. I don't know what happened either but I do know that I wasn't going to let him hurt you. The people I love will never be taken from me by another, again! Now let's get out of here, I'm going to be sick."

Dani helped Jenna off the table and put her shirt on Jenna's trembling, naked body.

"I have no idea where we are. How do we get out of here," Dani asked.

"Leave it to me," Jenna said as she held onto Dani. She clutched her tighter and closed her eyes and in an instant they were at the path of the Dark Forest. The sound of hooves galloped toward them and Mystery came out of the fog. Dani and Jenna had never been happier to see their beautiful horse. They helped each other onto her and she took off into the mist and back to the cottage.

16

"You blew up the god of Darkness!" Liza squealed in disbelief. " I want to do it next! Jenna, teach me how to blow up a god!

"Liza! Settle down. No one is blowing up anything, especially anymore gods. This was an accident and cannot happen again, right Danika?" Jenna said as she was explaining that evening's events to the coven members who she found waiting for her and Dani when they arrived at the cottage. The sisters explained that they could feel the danger that Jenna and Dani were in and came right to the cottage because none of them could scry their location. Anne Marie had done her best to give them all the information she could but there wasn't much to go on so they just waited there trying to reach them with their collective power. They had no luck. They were overjoyed to see them riding back to the cottage, somewhat in one piece. Now Jenna and Dani were giving them details of what happened.

"Nothing will get blown up as long as no one messes with my people," Dani answered, "and maybe now that message will be loud and clear."

"My concern is that there are other dark covens that are going to be chomping at the bit to get to Danika once news of this gets out. There has not been a power like this in a witch in a long time, especially one that has the added bonus of being the Archive," said Yvette.

"This is true. That kind of power combined with the knowledge is going to be too much for the malintent to resist," agreed Luzanna.

"It will be dangerous for all of you. I can feel the stirring of the darker forces as we speak," added Jean Renee.

"Danika has to leave, there's no way around it. The dark covens don't know which one of us is the Archive. We will all be in danger if they start trying to get to her by picking us off one by one. If she leaves right away, and goes far away they will only know that the field of power is gone and maybe we can spin this story somehow. Not too many people know of Danika's power and maybe with her away we can contain this; but she has to go right away," said Sara Jane, practical as ever and stating what everyone else was thinking but didn't want to say.

"Dani isn't going anywhere!" yelled Liza, "No one pushes my sister around, right Dani?"

Dani looked at Jenna and the look on her face confirmed that Sara Jane was right. There was no way around it; she had to leave.

"Liza, it will only be for a little while. Besides, you have to finish your training. You won't even know I'm gone. By the time you have figured out what your skills are and have developed them, I'll be back or maybe we will go somewhere different, who knows? The point is, it won't be forever. Plus, you are in great hands. You don't even know I'm in the room when Anne Marie is around."

"You're right!" Liza laughed as Anne Marie walked over to her and put her arm around her. "Just bring me something good from... well... where are you going to go?"

"Mexico!" Anne Marie blurted out. All the witches turned to her with quizzical looks. "There is the sweetest little boy who is telling me that you must go to Mexico. There is something there for you, people you are meant to help. This poor little child, he was only five years old when, nevermind. I believe what he says. You need to go to Mexico."

" I don't speak a word of Spanish but I do love that tequila. Okay, if you ladies think you will be safer with me gone, then I'll head southwest till things blow over. So mote it be!"

17

Danika loved getting on this bus and exploring the peaceful city. Her ride through the streets of Merida was a treat for the senses. The windows on the bus were open and a warm breeze carried in the smell of spices from the street vendors and restaurants they passed. The beautiful limestone buildings made everything look pristine and alive. There was music and singing coming from the park. Speaking of music, Dani had to stop at the local record store to get art supplies. It was a strange combination of items but this record store was her lifeline to all kinds of artistic endeavors. One part of the store sold records, instruments and all kinds of recording paraphernalia. The other side had a small but perfectly sourced section of art supplies. A very small part of the store contained herbs, oils and candles; pretty much one stop shopping for Dani. There was also all kinds of electronics and gaming stuff which she definitely had no interest in. Needless to say, the store was a bit cramped with stuff but when there weren't a lot of people in it, like today, then it wasn't too bad. She was on the hunt for an extra large canvas board. Too lazy to stretch her own she would purchase them here and have to lug the big thing home. This should be fun to fit on the bus, she thought to herself. After perusing the paints and brushes, which she talked herself out of buying because she had too much already, Dani grabbed her board. She paid the shopkeeper, who, Dani thought, she should be on a first name basis with, seeing she was in there at least once a week for the past year; but he was all business. Jose was a tall good looking kid, only eighteen, with shoulder length dark brown hair that always covered his face. Dani had to fight the urge to push it back behind his ear, but she didn't dare; she didn't want to act like his mother. They would chat sometimes and every once and a while she would even get a laugh out of him. Dani could tell he was an introvert and gave him credit for being out front dealing with the public; especially chatter boxes like her. Unfortunately for him, Dani was desperate for human contact and he spoke very good English. Canvas board in tow she was back on the bus. Dani gazed out the window at the shops and made a mental checklist of the ones she would want to come back to on her next trip.

Another thing Danika loved about her bus ride were the people she met. They were some of the most interesting and friendly people. The main purpose for her outing today was to buy art supplies but she also wanted to give Graziella the herbs she mixed for her to take for her arthritis. Graziella was the sweetest, little eighty year old lady who Dani had been talking to for weeks on this route. Unlike Jose, Dani and Graziella could chat up a storm. One time, they both missed their stops because they were engrossed in a conversation about cats! Graziella's English wasn't as good as Jose's, but that didn't matter when they were discussing creatures of the feline persuasion. Anyway, she would be getting on at the next stop and Dani was excited to see her. The herbs Dani mixed for her would make her feel like an eighteen year old. Mixing herbs for arthritis was nothing compared to the herb magic Dani practiced back home. Now that she was in self-inflicted exile, she had to keep things under the radar, and herbs for arthritis was common practice. Still, it was nice to be practicing something; to feel needed and to be helping people again, Dani thought.

Dani's thoughts were interrupted by an unusual noise. Was that gunfire? She had not heard that sound the entire year that she had been there. She couldn't believe she was hearing it now. Dani had picked the city Merida for her "vacation" because of its low crime rate and peaceful surroundings. She really needed to be somewhere where she wouldn't get involved… in things.

The gunfire was getting closer as the bus pulled to its next stop. The doors opened and, from her seat close to the front of the bus, Dani could see Graziella across the street. She was doing her best to duck down behind the mailbox, despite her arthritis. Dani looked down the aisle, out the back window. She could see the police in the distance. A bunch of people jumped on the bus, probably seeking shelter from the chaos. It had just gotten very crowded. The driver was about to close the door but one more person jumped in and the bus moved on.

There was little room now and that last passenger was standing right in front of Dani, holding on to the pole with one hand and his side with the other. She looked up slightly and saw blood starting to spread around his hand and through his fingers, soaking his shirt. Next to his hand she saw a very large gun tucked into his belt. He was who the police were after! He was a criminal; most likely a drug dealer, Dani thought. He was also really injured and needed help. She could not get involved in this, she tried to remind herself.

Dani looked up further and met his gaze, instantly losing her breath. She began to journey through his eyes, deep, deep brown. She could see everything in his eyes; his entire history, his connection to this part of the earth. He was heat. He was air. He was azure sky. He was danger. He was a child, a man, passion and energy; in control of all, yet helpless. She realized that he was staring back at her with a quizzical look. He had a slight smile on his lips. He was trying to figure out why she hadn't screamed yet, Dani thought. How could she scream? She was too busy trying to pull herself out of the vast pool of his eyes and wondering how that curl of his black, chin length hair was falling so perfectly in front of his beautiful face and…oh yes, how was she going to help him?

She reached into her bag and found the scarf that Graziella's herbs were wrapped in. She looked around and began to stand up from her seat. Everyone was too busy looking out the back of the bus to notice them. As she stood, she found herself about to be pressed against him but, before she was, she put her hand on his and slid the scarf between his hand and the bleeding wound. She stood now, pressed against him. Dani reached down behind her, grabbed her jacket and tied it around his slender waist to hide the bleeding, to hold the scarf in place and to put some pressure on it. Dani's eye level was at the top of his chest, right where his gold cross lay. She looked up at him and he was smiling a tight smile; but Dani noticed that his eyes were smiling even brighter than his strong handsome lips. The smell of him was intoxicating. It was the smell of some expensive cologne mixed with blood and the adrenaline of a predator who had no intention of being caught.

The bus came to a halt. A look back from the both of them to see that the police were in traffic behind them and some of them were jumping off their trucks, and taking to the street. Dani's wanted man reached for his gun. She grabbed his hand and gave him a slight shake of her head and motion toward the now open door. Some policemen were running down the street, through the stopped cars, toward the bus. There was chaos in the street now; gunfire, crashing, yelling and screaming. A motorcycle with two men on it flew by them. The man in back fired a machine gun at the police. The noise was deafening. The police were yelling at the bus driver not to move. They were checking all the stopped vehicles. Dani's fellow passengers were not waiting around to be checked over by the police and they were starting toward the front of the bus. Thinking quickly, Dani grabbed her very large canvas board and turned it across the aisle. This stopped everyone in their tracks putting them on one side and the mass of people on the other. She grabbed his hand and pulled him toward the door now using the canvas to somewhat hide them from the view of anyone coming toward them. As they descended the stairs, Dani pulled his arm downwards, signaling him to duck behind the canvas board. The police were getting closer but there were a lot of people and cars blocking the way. Dani and the young man were off the bus and crossing the street. She looked for Graziella and saw a woman helping Graziella into her house. Dani was relieved that she was safe.

The "fugitive" was now leaning, heavy, on her, his arm around her shoulder. She guided him down the street toward her apartment. They reached the doorway and Dani leaned her canvas against the wall of the hallway.

"Can you make it up three flights?" she asked him. She almost didn't expect him to answer her, mainly because she was speaking English but also because she thought that he must be from a dream that she was probably having right now.

"If I can't, I'm more than sure you will find a way to get me up there. You are as clever as you are beautiful," he answered.

He spoke English! His voice was like the smoothest tequila and she was completely on fire. Dani helped him up the stairs and wrestled with her keys as he leaned against the wall panting, trying not to look like he was losing pints of blood.

She helped him into her apartment. With a gesture of her hand, a few candles started to flicker. He noticed but, Dani thought, he was too weak to mention it. She walked him into the bedroom, flicked on a few more candles, and he slid off her onto the bed. She leaned over him and tore his shirt off and really wished that this was a completely different situation. Looking over his wound, she made a game plan of what herbs to pack it with after she took the bullet out. She wanted him up and about and infection free as soon as possible and the right mix would make that happen.

"Why are you helping me?" he asked.

"Well, let's just say that you are exactly my cup of tea. I absolutely love to save wounded animals that I find in the streets… or on buses."

She was very tempted to tell him that he was the most beautiful, wounded animal that she had ever saved, but held back.

"How do you know that I am not vicious or rabid?" With him she was more than willing to risk it, she thought to herself.

"I have a good sense about these things," she said to him.

She was sitting next to him on an ottoman by the bed, with one arm draped over his lap, her hand on his abdomen and her other hand on his bare chest. They were silent for a moment and she became trapped in his eyes, again. When he grinned at her it sent a shockwave through her and she removed herself from her position immediatly! She really needed to stay focused. I have a patient to operate on, she thought to herself.

Dani jumped up and moved across the room to her apothecary which was basically a table with fancy little boxes and small drawers full of herbs and things and trays of oils in colored glass bottles. She sparked on a few more candles and looked at him out of the corner of her eye to see his reaction. Nothing. He was leaning up on a pillow watching her every move, calm and trusting. She got to her work table but not before tripping over, one of her two, black cats. Quickly, the other arrived jumping onto the table to rub herself against Dani knocking all her stuff off the table. This, he reacted to, with a soft chuckle.

"They are beautiful," he said. "What are their names?"

"That chubby thing on the floor is Bast and this skinny girl here is Cleopatra. It's terrible but fat and skinny is the only way I can tell them apart. Oh, and Anubis is around here somewhere. He's a dog. Told you I like collecting strays."

She really needed to get to work; no more distractions. Dani started to feel like all she was, was distracted around this man and she wished that he would stop following her around the room with those eyes. Working around Cleopatra, Dani made a tincture that would put him out and numb the pain. Next, she made a poultice that she would pack his wound with. It would prevent infection and make him heal a whole lot faster. Walking back over to him, Dani grabbed a bottle of Tequila and handed it to him. He took a long drink.

As she gathered the things she needed, she laughed out loud at a thought she had.

"What is funny? he asked.

"When I take this bullet out of you I refuse to drop it into a metal tray! I could never figure out why they do that in the movies. That always annoyed me. We know the person has been shot and there is a bullet, and it is coming out! Why the metal tray? Why do they always have to prove that the bullet came out by clunking it into a metal tray? Annoying."

He stared at her a moment then burst out laughing. The sound of his laughter was pure magic; it was ethereal.

"Now that's what I call an opinion. I'd be afraid of you if you had an opinion on something really important!" he said through his laughter. He laughed a little more than winced in pain. Dani handed him the tincture.

"Okay, you're having too much fun being shot. Let's get this bullet out of you."

He laughed louder now and she assumed he was picturing her laying the bullet on a soft pillow after she removed it.

"Seriously, drink this and it will put you out for a few hours. When you wake up you will be good as new and then we will have plenty of time to joke around. You'll have to spend a few days here while you heal fully."

He gave her that tight lipped grin and smiling eyes, which, Dani now knew, had already endeared him to her forever.

Suddenly, a look of panic flashed over his face.

"My family needs to know that I'm okay! My mother will go crazy looking for me. I am very... important to her. I handle all her business." There was something very cold about that statement.

"And I assume she will be looking for you because you are her son and she loves you, as well?" she asked.

"No... I just handle her business." Dani had already wasted too much time now and really needed to get that bullet out. She was going to put whatever, that was, on the back burner for now, she thought to herself and handed him the tincture.

"Drink; when you wake and feel up to it you can call her." He grabbed her arm in desperation.

"You don't understand. She will burn this city down if she doesn't hear from me, and we cannot use your phone. I don't want them to come here. I don't want them to know where I am, just that I'm okay so she doesn't go crazy! I've been gone just long enough for her to start to panic and nothing good will come of it!" Geez, Dani thought, there is definately some dysfunction happening in that household but, none of this is my business. She began to feel really bad because he was visibly upset and she needed him to calm down if she was going to be able to remove that bullet.

"Drink this drink and I will take out the bullet. You sleep and I will go to the pay phone a few blocks away and call her. Tell me the number and I'll write it down". Hopefully that would relax him.

"Si, si, si. Perfect. You won't speak to her directly. Just speak to whoever answers the phone. Tell them the wolf strayed from the pack and is in a safe den; that he will make contact when ready. Don't say anything else and hang up."

"Ha," Dani laughed, "I told you I liked picking up wounded animals! I just didn't realize you were a wolf. I like it! It suits you."

"You have no idea." he said as he wrote down the phone number. "Promise me that you will make the call immediately after you are done here? I'm trusting you and I trust no one," he said in a chilling tone. She put her hand on his forehead, smoothed his hair back.

"I promise."

He drank the drink, closed his eyes, and was out. Time to go to work.

18

"Anubis, here!" Dani called her dog over and pointed to the floor next to the bed. "Protect him," she told him. Anubis sniffed her handsome patient, did a couple of circles, then plopped down on the floor next to the bed. With Anubis in charge Dani had no problem leaving the apartment. Anubis was no ordinary dog. He was a wolf/german shepherd hybrid. The dog was smarter than ninety percent of the people Dani knew. He took up half of her apartment and would defend her to his death, and Dani would do the same for him.

Dani threw on a light jacket and a pair of sneakers, locked the door behind her and went to find a payphone. Of course it has to be raining. It could be worse, she thought, it could be like the ice cold down pours we would get back home. This rain was more like a refreshing break from the heat. It was about ten o'clock. She looked around to see if police were still out on the streets after today's chaos. Sure enough she saw pairs of officers, here and there, patrolling. On a normal night there would only be a police officer at the station. Some stores were still open and people were gathered in little huddles talking about the day's events. In a few blocks Dani came to a pay phone. It was a bit beat up but it had a dial tone. She wasn't sure why but she was a little shaky putting in the change; she chalked it up to exhaustion and no lunch or dinner. That reminded her, he will be hungry when he wakes, so she should stop and get some food on the way home. The phone was ringing. Someone picked up but didn't answer. Dani was about to recite her lines but realized that her Spanish wasn't great and even worse when she was nervous. When she spoke it came out in English.

"The wolf strayed from the pack. He is safe in a den. He will make contact when ready." It was silent for a moment then there was a reply in English

"You are on a pay phone, yes?"

"Yes," Dani replied.

"Purchase a burner. Bring it to him." they said, then hung up. It took Dani a second to process that. She realized they meant for her to get him a cell phone. Got it. Off I go to the corner store to get some food and a "burner". Mission accomplished, Dani thought, proudly, to herself.

Back at the apartment, Dani put the food away in the fridge. She felt too exhausted to eat and didn't think her patient was getting up anytime soon. She went to the bedroom and found Anubis curled up next to their guest who in turn had his arm wrapped around the big goofball. Actually, it was a perfectly adorable sight, and Dani hated to break it up, but she was not sleeping on the couch. She hated sleeping on the couch! She had no problem sleeping next to a perfect stranger, especially one as perfect as this one, but she would not sleep on that lumpy couch. Dani giggled to herself because she knew that the couch was not that lumpy. She whispered loudly, "Beat it, Nubi." He grunts his annoyance then slid off the bed and over to the couch in the small living room. The cats quickly came out of hiding and jumped up on him as soon as he got comfortable, then proceeded to make themselves comfortable on him.

"Buenas Noches my friends," Dani whispered.

Back in the bedroom Dani fumbled through her drawer for a dry T-shirt and a pair of underwear and did a quick change. She looked over at sleeping beauty. I did a damn fine job on that stitching, if I do say so, she thought. While she admired her handy work she realized that he still had his pants and shoes on. Hmm, I've gotta do something about this, haven't I, she thought. She walked over to him. He was really out cold from the tincture she gave him. She removed his fine Italian leather shoes. No socks. Beautiful, long slender feet. She softly moved her hand over the top of one. Now, in the guise of checking his stitches, she slowly ran a finger from his chest, down the center of his abs and across the rim of his pants. She pretended to try and separate his pants from his underwear. Yup, just gently feeling around. Not too low; Just feeling the soft hair just under his lower abs. Darn it; found the underwear. She removed his pants. He was wearing black Y-fronts and it was really sexy. Of course she had to lightly run a hand over one of his well muscled legs. I really need to stop this, it's starting to feel illegal and I'm not the criminal here, Dani chastised herself.

She walked around to the other side of the bed and got in. Lying down facing him, she watched him sleep for a little while. She couldn't believe how attracted she was to him. She had never felt like this about anyone, nevermind that he was a complete stranger, and what she did know about him wasn't good. At this moment, Dani felt that this was where she wanted to be, by his side, for the rest of her long life. Unfortunately, she thought, he will be gone in a few days. There was no way that they could be together. We are from two different universes. I'm only hiding out in his, temporarily. These thoughts were starting to make her feel really bad. She needed to be closer to him. She gently moved her body against his. She put her head under his arm and against his chest and carefully put her leg across his and touched her feet to his. This was it, she thought. She wanted to be closer with all her heart, but this was it. At least he was hers for tonight and, the gods willing, a couple more days while he was hiding out. Here lies a couple of fugitives, she laughed to herself, then fell asleep listening to his heartbeat.

The next morning Javier was starting to come around after being in a very deep sleep. He spent some of it having his usual round of recurring nightmares. But just before he woke, he was dreaming of being eaten alive by a lion. That was a new one to add to the list of his disturbing dreams. Before he opened his eyes he could feel a warm body in his arm. He felt the softest skin he had ever felt. Then he felt something eating his foot. He opened his eyes and looked down at his feet to find one of them being gently gnawed on by a giant wolf; an actual wolf!

"Yeah, he does that, sorry. Anubis, knock it off," a voice with a thick British accent said. The wolf grunted, gave Javier's foot one more lick with his giant tongue, then sauntered away and laid down on the floor. Javier was pretty sure he was still dreaming. He looked down to see the woman from the bus, lying in his arms. The woman who saved his life. In this morning light and without being in severe pain, he could now see that she was even more beautiful than he thought she was when he first saw her. He looked deep into her hazel green eyes. They made him feel as if he were in a forest. She had long silky brown hair that fell to her hips and now cascaded behind her on the bed. His hand was on the leg that she had draped over his and he could not help but to move his hand back and forth to feel its warmth. She was not a dream. She was real and she was here lying in his arms. How did he end up here, in heaven with an angel, after the way the day had gone yesterday. Here's to fucking up, Javier thought.

"Shall I give you a recap of the evening after you passed out?" she asked. Javier felt a twinge of panic when he recalled his last thought from the previous evening.

"It's all taken care of, don't worry," she said as she put her hand gently on his cheek and caressed it. Her voice was soothing, like the purr of a kitten. " Your bullet popped right out. I didn't have to dig for it at all. Lucky for you, I'm an excellent seamstress," she giggled. He looked over at his side and felt it with his fingers. He was impressed. That would be one of his scars that would actually heal nicely.

"I called the number and told them exactly what you told me to say; about the wolf and the den and all. The man on the phone told me to get you a burner, which I did, so you can call your people when you are ready. Until then you are my prisoner and I've got the muscle to back me up," she nodded at Anubis who was now spread eagle on his back, basking in the morning sun. They both laughed. When they stopped laughing they just stared at each other; their faces inches apart. The desire in the atmosphere was tangible. A kiss was inevitable. The smell of him was like chocolate, she thought. You can't smell it and not eat it. He was moving his hand slowly up and down her soft thigh. She was like the finest silk, he thought, and couldn't help but wonder if she felt the same way inside. He leaned in and their lips gently interlocked. The kiss became stronger and desperate to become more than it could be. He turned on his side in an attempt to move on top of her and he breathed in sharply; not from pleasure but from the pain in his side. She gently pushed him back with one hand and removed her panties with the other. She put her hand in his underwear and felt his hard readiness. She slid down his underwear and held him, squeezing and stroking. She put her mouth on him and outlined every part of him with her tongue. Desperate not to lose control he grabbed her and pulled her on top of him and put himself inside her. She leaned over and whispered in his ear, "Don't move." She rose up, took his hands and placed them on her breast then started to ride him; up and down, faster and slower, grinding back and forth, reaching behind and between his legs to grab and feel handfuls of the rest of him. He watched her in ecstasy. He could see pink and red light glowing all around her. She was in her own world of pleasure, filled with him, one with him. He watched as long as he could before they both released themselves in an explosion of glorious sensation that they thought would explode the world around them. She gently collapsed on top of him and slid over to his side. He kissed her head and stroked her silky hair as it covered the both of them like a blanket. He had never been with anyone like this before. She was magic and she was now his. They slept this way until the evening.

19

Danika opened her eyes to find herself in her bed, naked. She looked at the clock and saw that it was eight o'clock in the evening. She had slept all day! Well, not all day, she thought to herself as she remembered her morning adventure. She could still feel him inside her. Where was he? She jumped up, grabbed her robe and went into the living room. She found her guest wearing nothing but a pair of her pink ruffled shorts. He was in the galley kitchen cooking for an audience of one dog and two cats. The animals were too busy eating huevos rancheros to pay any attention to her. He turned around with a frying pan full of delicious smelling eggs. When he saw her, the tandem smile of his lips and his eyes exploded onto his face. He dropped the frying pan on the counter and walked, quickly, over to her. He hugged her tightly then looked down at her and asked in his velvet voice, "What is your name?"

"Danika," she responded as a joyous feeling arose in her belly. "And yours?" she asked in return.

"Javier Jose Manuel Arturo," he retorted then began kissing her neck. "It Is my honor to make your acquaintance. I thank you for saving my life. I am madly in love with you and I am ready to take a place next to the mighty Anubis and never leave your side for the rest of our lives," Javier proclaimed. Anubis looked up from his eggs when he heard his name, then over at Dani, with a tilted head and a look of concern. Dani stood there completely overwhelmed. The words she just heard were everything she wanted to hear and everything she wanted to say back to him, but she knew one of them had to stay sane. He kissed her again and sat her down at the counter and served her breakfast; the whole time wearing nothing but a boyish grin and pink ruffled shorts.

"So, Javier," she began and was interrupted.

"Javi, my friends call me Javi. And since you are the love of my life, you can definitely call me Javi," he said. She pretended to ignore that and continued.

"So Javi, what is the plan?"

"Well, Danika," he answered, " for the first time in my life I am on vacation and I plan on spending it here making love to you and getting to know everything about you. So far I know that you are cunning and intelligent. You love animals. You, obviously, are not from this part of town. You appear to be an artist. You are a bruja. Hmm, and you are the sexiest most beautiful woman I have ever met."

"My friends call me Dani, and if you are going to be making love to me all week, then I think you should call me Dani," she said.

"Javi and Dani; perfecto, no? Eat. I'm a very good cook. My huevos rancheros are renowned," he responded. Dani was trying hard to be serious but really couldn't with him smiling that smile and trying to shove eggs into her mouth. She shut up and ate breakfast. He really was a good cook! Is there anything about this man she didn't like? Oh yeah, he's from some big cartel family and probably kills people for a living! What is happening, she asked herself.

As Dani finished her eggs Javi opened a bottle of tequila and grabbed a couple of glasses. She was about to complain about the inappropriateness of drinking tequila in the morning but realized it was eight thirty at night. He walked around the counter, took her by the hand and led her over to the couch. They sat down and Javi pulled two candles over, near the tequila and glasses. He looked at her then nodded his head in the direction of the candles. He wanted to see her magic. Dani flicked her finger at them and the flame began to flicker.

"You are unnervingly comfortable with my...abilities," said Dani.

"I've seen things," explained Javier, " In my line of work people do all kinds of things to get a leg up on the competition. My mother has a bruja in her employ. I'm not sure if anything she has done has affected our business, one way or another, but I wouldn't doubt it. Also, I'm pretty sure my mother sold her soul to the devil a long time ago. I think she gave him mine as a bonus. I pray everyday to my Jesus to find my soul and to save me from my sins. But now that I've met you, I may have been set free. Perhaps he has sent you to be my guardian angel."

"Yeah, I'm no angel," Danika replied, " and being a bruja, doesn't have to involve the devil."

"You certainly were no angel this morning," he said in a husky whisper as he took her glass from her and put it on the table. He then put his body on top of her and kissed her. She wondered how many times a witch could be set on fire this way and keep coming back. That thought was definitely in poor taste; yet here she was again, with him using her own body's senses as kindling, setting her ablaze and begging for his body to extinguish the inferno. He kissed and licked her neck then started on her breast. He squeezed and teased one breast with his strong hand, and sucked and flicked his tongue around the other's nipple. Her head was above his and she held onto him by his dark, wavy hair. As he suckled her breast his hand found its way between her legs. His long, skilled fingers felt their way through her curls, rubbing and squeezing. His thumb began a sensual circular motion around the perfect spot. He circled and circled, faster and faster; and sucked her nipple harder. She arched her back in ecstasy and let out a scream of absolute pleasure. It was over. She was on the couch trying to come back to reality, trying to catch her breath, feeling her heart rate coming down. She looked over at Javier to find him on the floor, pinned under Anubis who was waiting for her command.

"It's gonna take more than huevos rancheros to get him on your side, ya know," Dani said to him. There was that smile followed by a loud laugh, then a howl. Javi rubbed Nubi's ears with both hands and the very large dog flopped over for belly rubs which were forthcoming. The boys rolled around on the ground, bonding, while Dani laughed at them and drank her tequila.

The rest of the night was spent in the bedroom where the two lovers explored every inch of each other until exhaustion took them and they slept. It was the most peaceful sleep either of them had had in years. This night they were free from the nightmares of their youth that had plagued them both. They were sharing a serenity they never thought they would ever have again.

The next morning, Dani was the first to rise. She snuck out of the apartment to take Anubis for a walk. When she came back she found French toast on the counter and Javier on the burner phone. He was in her sheer black robe and nothing else. She really needed to get him some close she thought to herself, not that she minded this look on him. He held the phone to his ear with one hand and chewed at the thumb on his other hand. His head was down, his hair parted down the middle and draped his face in dark waves as he paced back and forth, listening to the voice on the phone. She sat and ate the best french toast she ever tasted and watched him listening intently to the caller. When he was done he put the phone on the counter then walked behind her and put his arms around her and his head down on her head.

"Bad news?" she asked.

"I just got an update on things," he said. "She told them to get me back immediately, but I told them to tell her it wasn't safe yet. I bought myself a few more days. Now what shall we do to pass the time?" he asked as he slid his hand inside her shirt and expertly fondled her breast. Dani grabbed his hand and turned toward him and looked at him with a very serious expression.

"What happens when your vacation is over?" she asked.

"Well, I thought about building you an amazing house. We can put a zoo in it if you want to. I will have to figure out where we can build it so she won't find you; somewhere close to me but somewhere where she would never think to look," he went on, excitedly.

"What happens if she finds me?" Dani asked. "What does she do, kill all your girlfriends?" she added, jokingly.

"Yes," he replied, "a couple she did herself, I was told, with her bare hands. Those two were the ones I thought I could be in love with. So, I just stopped being in love. I would just go out and have a fuck, here and there, when I needed to." Danika was speechless for a moment while she absorbed what he was saying.

"Does she love you so much that she doesn't want you to love anyone but her?" she asked. Javier threw his head back and laughed, an almost hysterical laugh.

"Oh my God, Dani, no! She hates me. She has hated me since the day I was born. The torture didn't start untill my father and brother were killed. Then she made my life a real hell. She turned me into a killer and as long as I'm doing that for her, she is happy. She leaves me alone when I'm doing my work for her. She respects the way I conduct business and she is smart enough not to spite herself. So I learned to enjoy my job well. I protect her, I'm in charge of her empire and I kill people she wants killed." Dani couldn't believe that his story just kept getting worse.

"Were you responsible for your father and brother's deaths?" she asked.

"I was ten years old. I was playing soccer with another boy. In her eyes, I didn't protect them. I betrayed the family. I know that's ridiculous; what could a ten year old boy do? I've come to realize that she wanted a reason to hate me and someone other than herself to blame for their deaths. It was her way to have control over me. When I was young I had no choice about the path that she put me on and now that I am older, it is all I know. I'm thoroughly trapped. If I show any affection to anyone, well, they're not around for long. She doesn't want anyone to free me of her," he explained. He sat, thinking for a moment then looked up at her, a plea in his big, beautiful brown eyes.

"You have power, Dani. I don't know what it is but I can feel it in you. You are like no one I've ever met. You are stronger than her, I just know it. Do you have the kind of power that would protect you from your enemies? I know that we have just met, but I am in love with you which makes her your enemy. I swore to never put any woman in that position again but I have no choice here Dani. I love you. I want us to be together, and we can't be as long as she is alive. She has controlled me my entire life. I've never had the will or a reason to try and get away from her. I now have a reason. You are my reason." She put her hand on his chest and could feel the love that he professed to her, inside him. She could also feel an ache in her heart for the pain he had collected.

"I need time to process all this. For one thing, I'm in hiding already. It's crazy for me to go into hiding in the place that I'm already hiding in…if that makes any sense? Another thing is that I am not a killer. I will protect you from her but I can't kill her." She lifted his face with her hands and kissed gently on his forehead, then his cheeks, his nose and his lips.

"You are mine now. I found you bleeding in the street and I'm keeping you. I'll go up against a monster for you. I won't let anyone hurt you. I would love to be the one to set you free of this way of life. But, let's come up with a plan first."

20

The next few days Danika and Javier spent all their time getting to know each other. Dani told Javi about her initiation into the craft and about being the Archive. She decided not to tell him about her extra long lifespan because it might be hard for him to wrap his head around that idea. She was still trying to understand it herself. She told him about her parent's death and the Coven of Darkness. Dani also told him all about her sister Liza and Jenna, who was as much a real sister to her as Liza. Javier told Dani everything he could remember about the day his father and brother were killed; about the little boy in the well and Don Pascal. When he talked about the little boy he cried tears of pain and Dani held him as he sobbed. As she held him she could see clearly into his memories. She saw the horror that was there and the things his mother had done and made him do. Dani started to understand why a grown man, especially one who seemed so strong and capable, couldn't break free of his mother. Dani almost started to feel intimidated by his mother herself but decided to shake that feeling off because she needed to be strong for him and would not add any fuel to the fear he already felt. Dani knew that this woman was going to be some kind of terrible to deal with but then again, Dani had dealt with evil before and came out on top.

Late afternoon Dani went out to get groceries and a few articles of clothing for Javi. Him roaming around the house in her underthings was starting to drive her wild. As she crossed the street to her apartment Dani started to feel that rush of danger. As heavy as her bag of groceries was, she decided to walk past her building and around the block. Looking around as casually as she could, she couldn't spot any trouble. She started to panic at the thought that maybe the danger was already in the apartment. She ran into the building, up the stairs then burst into the apartment surprising Javi, Anubis, Bast and Cleopatra who were all squeezed onto the couch watching television. Dani was just about to laugh at herself and the funny faces coming from the couch when she saw a figure from the corner of her eye. It was a man with a very large gun that looked like it had silencer on it; not that she'd ever seen one in real life. Dani ran to the couch and sat on Javier and transported everyone on the couch away from the danger.

21

Javier and Anubis threw up, the cats gagged and Dani was trying to figure out where they were. She searched her mind to sum up where it had sent them in her panic. It seemed that they ended up in Jenna's distant family's house. Jenna had always made mention of the house that had been in her family for generations. Some members of her family had sailed over on the Mayflower and had settled on that land. The amazing Victorian house was built in the 1800s and had been added to over the years. It had been willed to Jenna when the last of her relatives had passed. Jenna had visited it a few times but had no desire to stay. She loved her cottage too much and this house was filled with some pesky ghost. Jenna decided to use it as a safe house for any witches in need, which Dani figured she was right now. So, she guessed she was in the right place.

"What the hell just happened?" Javi asked, completely bewildered.

"There was a man with a very large gun coming up the stairs and...I...I guess I panicked and I think I transported us... to Massachusetts."

"Why Massachusetts of all places? That's in the United States right? Boston Celtics and all that?"

"Yup, Boston Celtics. This is a safe house for the witches of my coven. It's been in Jenna's family for generations. Over the years she has drilled into my head that, if I ever needed a safe place to go, this was the place. I guess my subconscious took the initiative and transported us here when I saw the danger. I'm so sorry!" Dani looked at Javier with a pathetic look on her face.

"Sorry!" Javi shouted, "Are you kidding me! This is fantastic. They will never find me here. How would they even know where to begin to look? I think my vacation just got extended!" Javi grabbed Dani, picked her up and spun her around.

"You're not upset?" she asked meekly as he put her down and started kissing her neck.

"No, how could I be? We are together and that's all I want," he said in between kisses.

"What about your business? Are you worried about it at all?" Dani asked.

"Listen to me, all I want is to be with you. It would take a miracle for them to ever find me here and as long as you are safe, let her struggle without me. Maybe this is what will finally finish her. Without me protecting her, I'm sure one of her many enemies will take the opportunity to take her out. Let the chips fall where they may." Javi plopped himself down on the couch in relief and Bast jumped right in the center of his stomach causing him to wince from her heftiness landing on his healing wound. Dani took a seat next to him and lifted his head and placed it on her lap. She stroked his smooth forehead and his silky, dark hair. Could it be this easy, she thought to herself; pop down to Mexico, find her soulmate, then pop over to a completely safe place for the both of them and live happily ever after. At the moment she couldn't see a downside to any of this.

"Was that one of your mother's men back at my apartment?" Dani asked, trying to sort everything out.

"Her's or one of our many enemies. I don't care. There is nothing I need to worry about now that I'm out of Mexico," he said, seeming more unstressed than she had seen him. Until now, he always seemed to be thinking steps ahead of everything; always having one eye open for something bad to happen. Dani figured that was how he learned to survive doing what he did.

"There isn't anyone you should contact or would that just give them clues as to where you are?" she asked.

"No, no one. Oh fuck. Jose," he said, the stressed look creeping right back onto his face.

"Jose, who?" Dani asked.

"My son," Javi said as he rummaged through his pockets looking for the cell phone Dani had gotten him. "Will this thing work from here?" he asked, more panicked now.

"Yes, I think so. Your son?" she asked, totally taken by surprise at this turn of events. So much for happily ever after, not that she minded that he had a son but that there was a loose end that he would assuredly have to deal with.

"I will explain in a minute," he said as he dialed the phone. " Jose? It's me, Javi. Listen man, I had to go out of town, unexpectedly. My motorcycle is in the alley behind your shop. Late tonight, when no one is around, I want you to walk the bike a few blocks away and dump it in another alley. Do not let anyone see you. Also, check on the record side of the shop and find my gloves and my helmet. Throw them out with the bike. I don't want anyone who comes looking to find any trace that I was there, do you understand? No, you can't keep the bike. I'll buy you a bike when I come back, just do what I tell you and get rid of that one, okay? Remember, you don't know me, got it? Okay man, listen you're a good kid even though you can't play video games for shit. Same to you, punk. Okay, okay, I'll be back soon. Stay cool, bro. Bye." All this was said in Spanish which Dani could understand better than she could speak and she could tell how worried Javier was about this boy. Just then, something dawned on her.

"Oh my god, is Jose the boy who owns the record store?"

"Yes," Javi answered, shocked that she knew him.

"I shop at his store at least once a week for my art supplies and other things. He is a great kid. He is tough to get through to, but I've cracked him a few times. When he does talk he is very smart and he has a kind soul. I liked him the day I met him. He is your son! Now that I know it, he looks like you. Oh shit, your mother doesn't know about him. How does she not know?" Dani asked.

"No one but his grandmother and, now, you. You are the first person I have ever told that I have a son. Just saying it out loud terrifies me. His mother and I were just children when we met. She was a few years older than me. Things happened between us very innocently and naturally. She worked in our fields and I would go out there to hide sometimes. No one knew about her. Her mother had enough sense to hide her pregnancy from everyone, including me. For the longest time I thought that my mother had killed her because that is what happened to the other women I had been with. Her mother contacted me years later and told me she had died giving birth to Jose and she had raised him herself. She only contacted me because she was dying and she wanted him to be taken care of. She begged me not to tell him that I was his father and to never involve him in our business. I swore to her that I would never do that and that I would love him and keep him safe, from a distance."

"How did you know that she was telling the truth and not just trying to get money from you?" Dani asked.

"I only needed to look at him and I knew. I loved him from the second I saw him. He was pure. He was my blood, untouched by the filth and horror that I was raised in. It made me feel like I had a second chance, maybe to live through his eyes. I got to know him through his grandmother, secretly, of course. I took the greatest precautions to make sure my mother never found out about him. I knew he loved music and electronics so I bought the store and told his grandmother to send him there to work. He took over like he had run a business his whole life. When his grandmother died I sent the deed to the store, to him, and made it look like he inherited it somehow. He didn't ask too many questions. All he needed to know was that the deed had his name on it, cut and dry.

"When he first started there I had left Instructions for him to sell whatever he was interested in and gave him money to start up. He brought in all the records and all the gaming and electronics stuff. It used to be an art store but he couldn't be bothered to move the stuff out, he just moved the new stuff in." They both laughed. "I am so proud of how well he has done for himself."

"Does he know you are his father?" Dani asked.

"No. I never told him; to protect him. I couldn't stay away from him though. I needed to be with him so I started by going into the store to buy things and asked him all about the stuff that he is into like gaming and music. I got into it too so it doesn't look weird that I go there a lot. We usually hang out in the basement of the place. I helped him fix it up and it's really high tech down there. I even fixed it so he could lockdown in the basement in case any bad news showed up."

"We must go back then. I'm so sorry I took you away from him. Let's go back," Dani said, panicking.

"No, no, Dani. I talked to him. He will be fine. I have been so bewitched by you, I didn't think. I mean, he doesn't even know I'm his father. He has his own life. He is completely independent. Someday I will tell him and we will be a family. Maybe now I can offer him a mother as well," Javier said this as he turned to Dani, took her hand and kissed the inside of it. He looked into her eyes and when she looked back, she could see a future there.

22

The rest of the day they spent making the living room and the kitchen livable. This was a big Victorian house with many rooms which they decided to explore at another time. Javier looked around and found a generator and he got it running, then he went out and chopped some fresh wood for the wood stove and fireplace. Dani was inside dusting things off in the kitchen. It must have been sometime since any one was here, she thought to herself. As she cleaned, she found that this house was very appealing to her. She went upstairs and looked into the several rooms up there. One bedroom had things in it that led Dani to believe that this room had been inhabited not too long ago. It wasn't half as dusty as the other rooms. There was a large blanket on top of the beautifully elaborate four poster bed. When she removed it, there was a lovely bedspread, and the sheets seemed fairly clean; at least for tonight, anyway. She will search for fresh linens tomorrow. The room was really lavish. The furniture was all dark mahogany and elaborately carved. The curtains were thick, embroidered velvet. There was a gilded, standing dressing mirror and a few tall candelabras. On the dresser were colored glass bottles, a jewelry box and candles that had melted down. She opened one of the bottles and sniffed it. Just as she thought there was an herbal concoction of somesort; a tell-tale sign that one of the coven had stayed in this room. She opened another bottle and sniffed again. This one contained her favorite ylang ylang oil. She dabbed some on her wrists. The smell of the oil always brought to her a feeling of sensuality. She stood up and walked over to the window and drew back the curtains to let some light in. The room was even more beautiful. The wall paper was a lush lavender with a gold brocade pattern. There were a few gold framed paintings of beautiful, seductive women in various states of undress. Very sexy, Danika mused. She opened the top dresser drawer and found some nightgowns and lingerie. Between the sexy boudoir and the smell of the ylang ylang she just couldn't help but try something on. She pulled out a silky negligee. It was a blush colored, short silk dress with a sheer see through halter top and sheer panels down the sides; very French. Dani kicked off her sneakers then removed her pants and pulled off her shirt and bra. She grabbed the nighty and walked over to the standing mirror and tried it on. Perfect! It fit her like a glove. She then sat back down at the dressing table and began to brush her long, brown waist length hair with a sterling silver brush. She realized that she had never looked at herself this way before and to her own surprise she was pleased with what she saw. However, she began to feel like she wanted to be pleasing someone else.

Javier had taken Anubis and the cats outside. The cats found a hot spot on the pavement of the driveway and commenced sun bathing. Anubis decided to get some exercise and chased a couple of angry squirrels up a tree. Javi was stacking some of the firewood he had chopped when he saw the curtains draw back on one of the second floor windows. He stepped back a few feet and could see Dani. He waved to her but she had turned sideways and was doing something. Then he saw her remove her shirt exposing her perfect, white breast. Javier was instantly ignited. He was shocked at how quickly his body responded to the sight of her naked body. He watched her for a few more minutes then dumped the firewood and ran into the house. He flew up the stairs and started opening one door after another until he found her. She was still at the table brushing her hair.

"Ah, you must be the lady of the manor. I am your servant and I've come to collect my payment for chopping the firewood," Javi explained.

"Oh really, Sir, and what is your fee for such a service," Dani responded playfully.

"I'm sure we can come to some sort of arrangement," Javi responded as he walked behind her, took the hairbrush from her and started to brush her silken hair. They stared at each other through the mirror. The way he was looking at her through the glass was electrifying her. He slowly placed the brush on the table then forcefully grabbed a handful of her hair at the nape of her neck and pulled her head back. Now there was nothing in between their gazes and he stared directly into her eyes from his position of dominance above her. There was a nervousness that now mixed with the desire that she had for him, and she liked it. He leaned forward, still holding her by her hair, and lightly bit on her neck; barely keeping himself from sinking his teeth into her. Then he kissed and licked her neck, her shoulder. His other hand came up under her arm and latched on to her breast, tightly. He pulled her against him and explored the front of her body with one hand while keeping her pinned by her hair with the other. There were so many sensations happening to her body right now, that she could barely take it. Right then, Javier put his arm under her legs and lifted her up into his arms and carried her to the bed. He placed her down in front of him and he was between her legs. Javier looked directly into her eyes again and Danika saw the wolf. His eyes were the eyes of a predator admiring his prey; thinking of what a feast he was about to have and it made her crazy with lust for him. She yearned for him to sink his teeth into her. He took his shirt off. She undid his pants. He grabbed her under her knee and lifted her leg up and kissed and sucked the inside of her thigh working his way inward. Then he dove his tongue into her dark curls and between her lips and kissed and sucked and licked. Dani held on to his strong shoulder and entangled her fingers into the waves of his hair. This went on, for what seemed like an eternity, until he came up and gasped for well deserved air. His hair was wild and juice dripped from his red lips. The wolf leaned over his prey ready to give the last blow. He plunged himself into her deeper and deeper. He was hard and brutal and she could do nothing but absorb each thrust; and each thrust just pushed her deeper and deeper into an ecstatic frenzy. She wrapped her legs around him as tightly as she could and dug her fingers into his shoulders. He wrapped his arms around her and buried his face into her neck and thrust deeper and harder and faster. The both screamed in release and spasmed in waves of pleasure that neither of them had ever experienced.

They had slept, entangled in each other, for hours. Javier awoke with a chill. He moved Dani over onto a pillow and covered her. He put his pants on and went downstairs and out the kitchen door. Outside, he came face to face with a dog and two cats who looked like they were about to scold him but decided to give him the cold shoulder instead and walked past him into the house. Javier cringed a little at the fact that they had been forgotten about. He decided that he would make it up to them at breakfast. He got some firewood and went back into the house. The animals, as annoyed as they were, followed him up the stairs and into the bedroom. He started a fire in the fireplace then removed his clothes and climbed in bed and pulled the woman he loved into his arms. Anubis jumped into the nice warm spot that Dani had been in, followed by Bast then Cleopatra. Javi gave thanks for his new family and king sized beds.

The new family explored the house and the gardens. They had been living on some of the non perishable items that were in the pantry and some vegetables that were growing out in the huge garden. There was a pumpkin patch and Dani showed Javi how to carve one for Halloween. She explained all about Halloween and all its traditions and Javi, inturn, told her all about the Mexican Day of the Dead. Javi also showed off by carving three more pumpkins and they put them out on the front porch for display. They stood on the walkway to observe their handiwork. Javier had his arm around Dani and when she looked up at him, he looked down at her with that tight proud smile, accompanied by the smile in his eyes.

The day after Dani found a witch's dream come true herb garden that must have been added to each time a witch came to stay at the house. She found it because Bast and Cleo were rolling around and bounding in and out of the catnip that was one of the herbs planted there. It was a bit of a mess but nothing a little weeding couldn't help. There was an old car in the garage that Javi was going to try and get running. Once he did that, they would have to find a market and stock up. They were both enjoying playing house and being free from all of their responsibilities.

A few days later Dani and Javi decided to get away from the house for a while. Javi was extremely eager to get out until he actually got outside and was hit with a real New England autumn chill. They went back inside the house and up to the attic to see if there were any old sweaters or jackets put away. There were plenty of old things in the huge attic and they were able to rustle up some things that weren't completely moth eaten. There were so many antiques, Dani thought as she rifled through an old jewelry box.

"We are going to need to do some exploring in this big, old place," she said. Just then, Dani caught a glimpse of a little girl running behind a large armoire.

"What was that?" Javi shouted.

"Did you see her too," Dani asked.

"See who? No, something just pulled my hair," Javi answered as he rubbed his head. Dani looked up above him and saw a little boy peeking out from the rafters, giggling to himself.

"Alright, cheeky monkey, enough of that. There will be no hair pulling. Be nice and my friend and I will play with you when we get back," Dani said in a firm tone. She looked at Javi and said "Ghosts."

They found an old rope to tie around Anubis then headed down the long walk to the front gate. There they opened a very large, rickety wrought iron gate and continued down the street. It was a perfect fall day. Gorgeous leaves of red, orange and yellow trickled down from the tall trees. The sky was a beautiful shade of blue that made the orange in the trees look like an explosion. Javi had never seen an autumn like this. He was kicking the leaves and picking up special ones to keep, just like a child. He even got Anubis into the act by picking up handfuls of leaves and throwing them at him which Anubis would then try to jump at and catch. After a mile, they came to a main street that had a bunch of little shops. They stopped at a small restaurant that had some outdoor seating heated by an electric fire.

"I am starving! What should we have? I am totally out of my element now. Wait a minute, have you ever been to America?" Javi asked. Danika was looking over a menu.

"We are going to have lobster rolls and a beer and you will love it, and yes, I've been here several times. I haven't been to this house or part of Massachusetts but me and my coven have come to nearby Salem to meet with some very powerful witches. Jenna has a few relatives all over New England."

The food arrived and Javi dove into his sandwich.

"Dios mio, this is amazing," he proclaimed.

"Now follow that with a swig of beer," Dani recommended. Javi smiled that smile and Dani felt the heat then giggled at his childlike awe.

They finished their dinner, enjoyed another beer then strolled through the town. Things were decorated for Halloween. There were purple and orange lights tied around the street light poles and carved pumpkins on the doorsteps of the shops. Dani's interest was piqued by a quaint rare bookstore. The couple entered the store and looked around. Javier reached for a book, brought it down from the shelf and admired the fine old binding and fine parchment that the pages were made of. A short, balding man with thick glasses walked over to them.

"The gentleman has fine taste. That is a first edition Don Quixote; very fine, precious book. There are only three in existence," the shop-keeper said very smugly as he took the book from Javier and placed it back on the shelf.

"That is true, Senor," Javi said as he took the book back down from the shelf, "and if I purchase this one it will complete my collection. Would you kindly wrap it for me while we continue to rummage through your little shop. Gracias." Javi handed the book to the little man.

"Sir, this book cost $8000."

"Si Senor, and if you give us a few more minutes to browse, maybe we can add to that bill. A good day's profit for you, no?" The shop-keeper's glasses fogged with embarrassment as he waddled over to the front desk.

"That was brilliant!" Dani squealed as she buroughed her head into his chest so the man couldn't hear her giggle, "What a bloody little snob, assuming that we aren't the types to appreciate a rare book." Dani was quiet for a few moments.

" Okay, I'm a terrible hypocrite. I was shocked that you have a collection of rare books. How did you get into that, of all things," Dani asked, her own embarrassment showing.

"Well, I have always loved to read. Probably the only thing my mother did right by me was to give me an education. I escaped into books and stories when I was a kid; and quite honestly, as an adult as well. As an adult I have acquired a vast amount of money, somehow," he said slyly, " and I started to buy first editions of the ones I love. Don Quixote is one of my favorites. It just goes to show what luck you have brought me that I have found this copy in such a strange place. I would have never found it had I not been here with you," he leaned down and gave her lips a warm, gentle kiss," I hope I continue to impress you." Another kiss. At that moment Dani felt the rush, but it wasn't from Javi's amazing kisses. It was that feeling of impending danger rising within her. Dani could hear Anubis barking from where he was tied outside. The bell above the bookstore door rang and a woman in a brown tweed coat and brown hat walked in very quickly and rushed by Dani and pushed her right into Javier.

"Pardon me my dear," said the woman, "I just can't get used to these new glasses. I'm so sorry."

"No worries," Dani replied and noticed that the feeling of danger had subsided. She also noticed that Anubis had stopped barking as well. Perhaps something had gotten the dog riled up outside and Dani was tuning into what he was feeling. Whatever it was she was happy that it had passed because this was too good of a day for any kind of drama. Javier was still looking up and down the aisles now holding three more, probably, very expensive books. Dani was taking in the atmosphere of the store. She loved the warm yellow light that some lamps were throwing and the smell of the old books and antique furniture made her feel like she was back in England, in a castle's library. It was very dark out and Danika turned to speed Javier along when she saw the shopkeeper take a book from a safe in the wall, behind the counter. The book was wrapped in a black velvet cloth. He handed it to the woman in the hat and opened the cloth for her to see the book. At the same time they both turned their heads, abruptly in Dani's direction. The book fumbled out of the woman's hands and onto the counter, partially exposing it. Dani could clearly see that the book had an aura of red and black; the sign of a cursed object. The woman scrambled to cover the book and plunged it into the front of her coat then pushed past Dani, again, and out the door. Dani knew that that whole situation should be making her panic but she just didn't. She just wanted to get Javi and Anubis and go home. Luckily, Javi was placing his books on the counter and the man was quickly ringing him up. He seemed to want them out as much as Dani wanted to be out.

"That will be $15,050.00. Cash or card," asked the clerk, his glasses beginning to fog again.

"That will be my card, Senor, gracias," replied Javier.

They left the store with a hefty bag of books, untied Anubis and began the mile walk home. It was a beautiful fall night in New England. The street lights glowed yellow. Leaves cascaded down from the trees. All the fresh air was making the three of them ready for a good night's sleep. In a few minutes they would be home and could do just that.

23

As the trio approached the gate to the house Anubis began to growl softly and he looked very alert. He started to walk low to the ground at a slow pace and the ruff of fur on his back stood on end.

"Should we be concerned about that?" Javi asked Dani.

"No, he probably just spotted a squirrel, let him have at it." Javi wasn't so sure but he figured she knew the dog best and he dropped the leash. Anubis took off running past the gate into the shadows of some trees. They both heard a yelp. Javi looked at Dani who, very strangely, didn't seem concerned. His sense of danger was now on overload and, unfortunately, had been delayed by Danika's lack thereof. He started to go for his gun but, instead felt one in his back and he stopped. A man and a woman dressed in black had grabbed Danika, slapped tape over her mouth and were walking away with her. She was struggling to get away from them, but nothing else.

"Stay right where you are sir and hand me your weapon. We will explain everything once we've dealt with that fugitive," said the voice that belonged to the gun in his back.

"What do you mean fugitive, where are you taking her, who are you!" Javier demanded.

"F.B.I. sir. Walk with me to the house and I'll explain everything," the man in black said as he handcuffed Javier and walked him up the driveway.

The two men walked into the house and the one in black switched on the lights. He sat Javi in a chair and uncuffed one hand then cuffed it to the arm of the chair.

"What the hell is going on, you son of a bitch? If you hurt her I will kill you all! Javier hissed, now getting very angry with this strange feeling of being trapped.

"Kill me, Mr. Arturo? You should be thanking me. We just saved your ass from one of our most wanted fugitives. That little lady who is leading you around by the nose is one of the most elaborate fraudsters we've ever seen."

"Danika? You're out of your fucking mind!" Javi shouted, his anger building by the second.

"Does she have you believing that she is a witch?" the man asked, watching Javi's expression, which was one of complete surprise. How did they know, he thought to himself, shocked. "Ha, it's amazing to me how a pretty face can distract a man into stupidity. She's not a witch, she's a con artist. Did she do tricks like make candles light by themselves? Just ask yourself, did she give you anything to drink? Because that's what she does, she is a master in herbology and drugs all her victims. She gave you hallucinogens. Mixing herbs to make people see things and knock them out is what she does. If she were a witch, why didn't she stop us from taking her?" Javi looked up at the man showing him that he had been asking himself the same question. But he still could not believe any of this. He had no problem believing that Dani was a witch but all of this seemed ridiculous.

"How the hell do you explain how we all came here from Mexico then?" Javier said, feeling like there was no way this guy was going to rationalize that and if he didn't, Javi thought, he was going to kill him with his bare hands.

"What part of ' she drugs people' don't you understand? She posed as a doctor, which is part of her M.O. She put you in a wheelchair and told everyone that you were her patient, headed to the U.S to be put in a mental hospital. Gotta give her credit though, she draws up some pretty legit looking documents. Here's the passport she made for you," the man put the passport down on Javier's lap. " Like I said, she is very elaborate. She gives her victims sad back stories, like her parents were lost at sea on a ghost ship and her mother was eaten by crabs. Ha! I love that one! Her mother had cancer and her father died from Parkinson's disease! She knows how to get under men's skin, that's for sure."

"Why?" Javier asked in a whisper.

"What else? Money. She must have run out of marks here at home and decided to get some imported meat. So what does she bring home? A cartel heir. Who's got more money than you? She was probably gonna drain you for a while then do what she always does; make a disposal. That's why she had to sneak you out of Mexico. She wouldn't have been able to get away with it there with all your people around." The man sensed that Javi was convinced now. "Listen, we're not interested in you. We are going to let you go. Take that passport, head to Logan airport, go home and consider yourself lucky.

Imagine if that little thing had killed you and you didn't die full of bullets from a rival cartel; that would have been a shame." the man laughed.

"Fuck you," Javier retorted.

"There's your passport. I'm dropping the key over here and when I'm gone you can wiggle over here and uncuff yourself. Then you will go home if you don't want any repercussions. See, we're the good guys and you owe us one." The man threw the key down on the floor then turned around and walked out the front door.

Javier's head was spinning. Everything the man said made sense. He had really believed her. He wanted to believe her. He was the perfect mark for her story because he really needed someone with supernatural power to end his torment of a life. Was he that pathetic, he thought, that he could believe that she was a witch; to let himself be fooled so easily. He was devastated. He was heartbroken. He was leaving.

24

Here we go again, thought Danika. Once again she had been taken captive, tied up and brought underground. They had thrown her into a van and drove, not too far, to what looked like a large school. They took her inside and down several staircases and took an elevator down until they came to a series of tunnels. She was led through them then into a room where they sat her in a chair and, simply, handcuffed her to it. This is what Dani could not figure out. She knew that she could easily use her magic and remove the handcuffs in a flash but she had no desire to. She felt sick when she thought about not going after Anubis when she heard him yelp. Why would she not go after him? Why would she let them take her away from Javier? What have they done to him? Why didn't she do something?

Just as though she was secretly being studied and her mind read, came a voice from the dark.

"We drugged you. A tiny patch was put on the back of your hand at the bookstore and you have been rendered, shall we say, apathetic. You have no will or desire other than what we instruct you to do. Very clever if I do say so myself. Sometimes subtlety is the very best form of trickery."

"Who are you and what will you be instructing me to do?" Dani asked.

"We are the keepers of The Necronomicon," stated the voice as he and about twenty other figures came out of the shadows and formed a circle around her.

"You have got to be kidding," Dani responded with a chuckle, "The Necronomicon is a work of fiction you poor deluded little cult-lings!" she continued as she laughed some more. "You people have just kidnapped me and disrupted my life for a made up horror story. When, whatever the hell you gave me wears off, I am going to be seriously angry. The last person who pissed me off was a god and I blew him up!" Some of the cult members looked nervously at each other, intimidated by Dani's casual confidence.

"The Necronomicon is real and we have been waiting for a powerful being to help us access its power. We detected your arrival when we registered a power surge on the night you transported here. We knew that house was owned by witches. We have been watching it for years, waiting for a powerful witch to show up. When you got here, we did all our research on you and the Mexican; one of our members is a clairvoyant who can see clearly into one's past. Great for snooping!. Now that we caught you we will use you to read the book and give us its powers."

"Seriously, this is daft! Even if it's real, it is more than likely evil. It is the book of the dead. It makes its readers insane, which it has obviously done to you lot. What makes you think it will give you powers?"

"We are the ones who believed. We are the ones who searched after the legend and found the book, here in the catacombs of the college. We are the ones who were chosen to reap the rewards of its power."

As Dani looked around the dim lit room she started to see the faces of the members gathered. She surmised that they were, perhaps, students and some faculty of one, or maybe several, of the colleges nearby. Smart, stupid people, she thought to herself.

"You know what, I am so sure that your book is absolutely a piece of fiction and nothing more, that I am going to read it for you without a struggle. How would that suit you?"

"Why… just fine…thank you!" stuttered the leader. "Give us a minute to put on our ceremonial robes. Would you like a ceremonial robe?"

"No!" Danika snapped. "All I want to know is when this apathy potion will wear off."

"From what we researched, it should be worn off after twenty four hours," answered the cult leader.

"And what of the man I was with, what have you done with him," She asked.

"He will probably be on his way back to Mexico once Skeeter gets done with him. He posed as F.B.I. and told him you were one of America's most wanted," he laughed with a wheeze, "Oh and your dog is okay too, mild tranquilizer, sorry."

"Javier isn't going anywhere. He wouldn't believe a word of that," Dani said, starting to become annoyed, which she thought was a good sign that the drug was wearing off.

"I wouldn't be too sure, lady; Skeeter is a theater major, " and with that he turned and walked out the door followed by the rest in single file.

They returned in their ceremonial robes and rolled a book stand into the center of the room. On the stand was the book. The Necronomicon. Martin, as the leader was called, followed all the historical clues and found the book, bricked up in a wall, down here in the tunnels under an old bible college. It all had a ring of truth to the legend of where it was hidden. But, this was a book of fiction, not a book of spells, or a power like these people had deluded themselves into believing. At this point, Dani just wanted to get this over with and go home and be with Javier. They promised to let her go once it was over and they really had no way to stop her; especially when her powers were back. She actually felt a little bad for these guys because she was sure nothing was going to come of their quest. Martin uncuffed Danika and walked her over to the book.

"My fellow congregates, tonight is the night we have all waited for. It is the night that our bible will be read to us. This is our bible just as the great literary genius, H.P. Lovecraft is our holy father. He has left the keys to all the power of the universe in the pages of this grimoire, which this chosen being will read for us. In moments, we will become gods on earth and we will contain more knowledge and power than any humans on the planet; for we are the believers, our father's chosen disciples."

Very eloquent, Dani thought. Too bad they were going to be very disappointed. Martin stepped aside for Danika to stand in front of the podium. She took a look at all the folks in their fancy dress, so full of hope and, unfortunately, about to get their dreams smashed.

Dani looked at the closed book in front of her. They say that the binding is made of human skin and written in blood. From the look of it, she thought that might be true. She was ready to begin. She opened the book. The ground began to vibrate, then shake. The congregation started to panic but Martin silenced them and nudged Dani to continue. The earth shaking is usually not a good sign when it comes to supernatural items and Dani was starting to rethink this, but it was too late. When her eyes finally rested upon the first word on the first page, it came off the page and was absorbed into Dani's eyes, into her mind and into the Archive. It was then followed by each successive word until they all vanished from the pages. The pages in turn disintegrated. Dani felt a surge of power rush through her and her eyes glowed white. She could almost sense the thoughts from the book finding their places in the archive inside her. Martin and his gang were right about the book; it did have power. Unfortunately for them they chose a witch who was an Archive, and sacred knowledge like what was in that book desires to be hidden in just such a place.

When the book was done, Danika opened her eyes. All the cult members, except Martin, had fled.

"What did you do to my book," he sobbed.

"It wasn't me, it was the book. It never wanted to be found. The secrets in it were never meant to be spoken, much less written and compiled. Whether Lovecraft made it all up or had access to some reckless god that tried to leak forbidden knowledge to an inapt world, we will never know, but the knowledge was real. You were right about that. But be grateful that you did not access it because it would have blown your's and all your pal's heads off. You may not think it now, but it was a good thing you picked me and not some other witch. Take my advice, go back to school and make tomorrow the first day of the rest of your life and get your knowledge the old fashioned way." With that Danika walked over to the elevator and got in. "Are you coming, Martin?" she asked the fallen leader. He picked up a hand full of ashes then watched them as they blew out of his hand into nothingness. He turned and got on the elevator. As the doors closed Danika put her arm on his shoulders and he dejectedly put leaned his head on her.

"I'm really sorry about all this," he said sincerely, "my gosh, we outright kidnapped you, we drug darted your dog and we chased your boyfriend away. He's probably half way back to Mexico by now. I was mad with power and now that the book is gone, I don't feel any of that obsession. I'm very disappointed with myself as a human being."

"It's not completely your fault, Martin. Supernatural items like that book aren't meant for just anybody. Some humans are born with a special connection to the spiritual realm, like witches, mediums, and empaths and many other kinds of people with special gifts. Some objects are infused with entities that have broken free from realms that they shouldn't have broken free from and need to be contained. I think that's what the Necronomicon was. It possessed you. I contained it. That's sort of my thing; I'm like a vault. So in a way, It was good that you used me to try to open the book's power instead of anyone else. Who knows what would have happened. Don't be too hard on yourself, just don't do anything like that again."

"Do you want me to try to contact your friend and explain? It's the least I could do."

"No, Martin, Not necessary. He wouldn't believe anything your guy told him. I'm sure he's pacing the floors at home trying to think of how to rescue me. Oh, and about kidnapping me, don't worry about that either; it happens to me all the time," Danika laughed as she and Martin stepped off the elevator, walked out of the building and into the morning sun.

25

"Javier! Javier!" Danika shouted as she ran through the doors of the grand Victorian. There was no answer. She ran down the foyer, looked into the main living room then ran into the kitchen. Nothing. She opened the backdoor of the kitchen that led to the side yard and called again. No response. Dani ran back in and was about to climb the stairs to the bedrooms when she heard voices coming from the cozy sitting room next to the library. She ran in.

"Javier!"

He was not there, but, to her surprise, there were four girls sitting on the floor, and Anubis who was lying in the center of them.

"Who are you?" Dani asked, quite shocked.

"Who are you?" one of them snapped back.

"I'm Danika and I belong here; and that is my dog. Oh my god, did you give him a bath, and is he wearing a chain of flowers? What the hell is going on?" Danika demanded.

"Calm down lady. We belong here too. We are starting a coven and we've come here to gather herbs and train. That's what this house is for, isn't it? We found this poor dog unconscious in the cold wet grass when we got here last night. We were in the garden picking night plants under moonlight and that's how we spotted him. We woke him up and he was dirty and shivering so we put him in a hot bath."

"I'm sorry girls, I've had a horrible evening battling an evil cult."

"That must have been the power surge Ami sensed last night," one of the girls responded. With that, Dani knew these girls were the real deal.

"What are your names," she asked as she plopped down in a large wingback chair. Anubis lazily got up and sauntered over to her and laid his giant head in her lap. He seemed to be forgiving her for last night and apologizing for having so much fun with his new friends that he had forgotten about her for a little while. Bast and Cleopatra came out of hiding and jumped up on her lap as well and nuzzled her face.

The smallest one, who had pretty auburn hair and glasses gave the introductions.

"I'm Ali, that's my sister Emi, that's Ami and she's Tay," The little one said with authority.

Danika took a good look at the future of witchcraft in America. Ali was a little spit fire and probably was the leader because no one was going to tell her otherwise. She could tell Ali was extremely intelligent, Her sister, Emi, was a tall, pale blonde beauty, with a quiet, shy disposition; definitely an empath. The oldest of the group was Ami. She was heavily tattooed with some beautiful artwork and seemed to be the mother of the bunch. Danika could feel the catlike caution that she was using to detect friend or foe. Ami seemed quite sweet but quite dangerous at the same time. She had the makings of a powerful witch. Lastly, there was Tay. She wore glasses that covered beautiful blue eyes and seemed to be the creative force of the group. She was in a pile of sketches of Anubis and was now busy sketching Dani. The sketches looked as if they would walk off the pages. Danika liked these girls already.

"Ali, Emi, Ami and Tay. That sounds like an incantation to me. I'm Danika, this big fellow who you've already met is Anubis and these two ladies are Bast and Cleopatra. Javier, my friend will be here as well, as soon as I can figure out where he went. I hope you don't mind sharing the accommodations with us. We will stay at one end of the house. Maybe I can teach you all a few things." The girls got very excited.

"That would be amazballs!" Ali said as she jumped up and around the room.

"The man isn't here," Emi interjected, softly. "He left last night. We were hiding in the bushes, trying to see who was in the house. A man in black left first. Then your friend was in the house alone. He was very angry. I could feel his anger and disappointment building up as he sat in the dark trying to figure out what to do then he stormed out of the house. I think he went home. That's what I felt from him."

Danika was dumbstruck. He actually left her! So much for her soulmate. One bucket of lies and he was out the door.

"Thank you for that, Emi," Dani said trying to hold back her tears as they welled up in her throat. If you ladies don't mind, I'm going to go up stairs and rest for a while. I've had a very bad night." Emi put her soft hand on Dani's and looked at her with her pale blue eyes, and the pain that Dani was feeling, reflected back at her. Danika jumped up from the chair and ran upstairs.

She flung herself on the bed and sobbed. When she caught the scent of him on the sheets she cried harder. How could he leave her? He loved her. She knew he did. No lie that they could have told him should have shaken his faith in her. They were soulmates. She knew this to be true. So how could he have left her so easily.

"It's not always all about you, you know," Jenna said to her after appearing, sitting in the chair in the corner of the bedroom.

"I don't want to hear from the voice of reason right now! I just want to cry till my eyes bleed if that's alright with you!" screamed Danika.

"Is that anyway to speak to your dearest friend, who felt your heart break as if it were her own and came running to you from across the sea?" Jenna chided her as she walked over to the bed and sat by her side.

"Just what I need! A guilt trip! I'm sorry my heart breaking inconvenienced you," replied Dani who sobbed even harder now.

"Alright, alright," Jenna said, realizing that trying to snap her out of this wasn't going to work. She handed Dani a tissue and stroked her head. "I'm sorry, love. Why must all your life experiences be learned the hard way? Here you've met your true love and he is your first love. You poor dear, you have no experience in love, nevermind the love of a soulmate; and one as damaged as yours, to boot. You are very lucky and very unlucky at the same time. Do you understand what I mean?"

" I guess so. This would be easier if I had something to compare it to," Dani answered, between sobs.

" And you would know that the harder you love the more painful the heartache."

" How do you know Javier is damaged? I mean I know he is, but how do you know?"

"Your sister, Liza, has mastered scrying. She watches the mirror like it's television. I have to keep tabs on her because she is very nosy. She's been reprimanded more than once. I'm trying to teach her to use her gift in constructive ways but she is just too good at it. It takes her seconds to conjure a picture. You should have a talk with her when you see her because she is always spying on you, mostly because she misses you but also because she's a little imp," Jenna giggled. Dani chuckled as well. She turned over on her back and stared at the ceiling.

"What am I supposed to do now? I feel numb. I feel like everything was perfect. We were planning a life together and he just ran away."

"There's no way the two of you can start a life together until he deals with the person who has him in chains. It's not just him who needs to be set free, either. Go to him. Help him and you will help many. Balance will be restored."

"That is extraordinarily cryptic, Jenna," Danika said, now sitting up on the bed and starting to feel motivated.

"Go to him. Go back to Mexico and announce to all involved that he is yours. Then ask him why he really left." With that, Jenna kissed Danika on the forehead and disappeared.

Jenna was right, thought Dani. She loved him, she knew he loved her and she wasn't going to let anyone or anything get in the way of that. She was surprised at herself. She could fight evil gods and cursed objects and misguided cults but she curled up and cried like a schoolgirl when faced with one obstacle that threatened her heart. Nope! No more! No more crying; time to go back to Mexico and get her man.

26

She flung open the large iron gates of the compound as if they were curtains and walked through them, in command and determined. She wore a share black shirt, black wide legged pants and black high heeled shoes. This was her power suit, she thought as she dressed that morning. She was going in like a boss so she would dress like a boss. Today she was going to get what she wanted. She was sick of being used by people, taken by people and manipulated by people. She wanted him, she was taking him back with her and she was going to face all obstacles head on.

She walked straight down the path with a wide confident stride, her long, straight hair flowing behind her in the breeze. There were dozens of men who protected the compound and they were finding themselves rendered immobile. They couldn't move, or shoot or speak. Dani strode right past each of them, straight up to the veranda of a gorgeous mansion where La Madre stood waiting for her.

"I assume you are who my son was distracting himself with. I am his mother Suzanna Rosa Arturo. Please, won't you come in," said La Madre as she held her arm out towards the entrance welcoming Danika into her home. Danika looked her over first. She was a tall, intimidating looking woman. She had an aura of power about her, but nothing supernatural; just pure human cruelty. She had perfectly coiffed black shoulder length hair, tan skin, black eyes and deep red lips and fingernails. She was wearing her power suit which, ironically, was all white. Dani couldn't help thinking that they were like two queens on a chess board. Dani also felt as if La Madre had been expecting her. She lifted her chin and marched into the house.

"Please have a seat," said La Madre like a charming hostess would, "what shall I call you, my dear."

"My name is Danika Devlin. Call Me Danika."

"What a lovely accent you have. You are British?"

"Thank you, I am from Cornwall; Tintagel Castle, King Arthur and all that. You speak English beautifully. I'm afraid my Spanish is nowhere near as good as your English. Wait, you spoke English to me right away. How did you know?" Dani asked, already on high alert with this woman.

"Javier made mention of it. Of course I had to find out what or who could have possibly kept him from his work for so long. He is very serious about his business and we were all shocked when he didn't come home after his little skirmish in Merida."

"You keep saying his business; don't you mean your drug empire?" Dani taunted, wanting to get down to brass tacks.

"You are mistaken, my dear. I am just a figurehead. It was my husband's business and when he was killed I tried everything I could to keep Javier from it but when he was old enough his uncle, Francisco, made sure that Javier followed in his father's footsteps.

"I am very interested in how you got my men to let you walk right into this, usually, impenetrable fortress. Did you use some kind of mind control or how do they say, telekinesis? I'm sure Javier would find that quite useful when dealing with his many enemies. Is that why he had you come here?"

Boy, Dani thought, this really was a chess match and she wasn't believing anything that came out of this snake's mouth. Was she really trying to get her to believe that Javier was the kingpin here and that she was an innocent bystander? The figurehead; ha!

"I came here because I am in love with Javier and we are going to be together. As soon as he comes back we are going to talk some things over and then we are going to leave this place."

"You may think you love him, my dear, as he can be quite charming but he is a cold blooded killer and the only thing he loves is money and power. That is probably why he is leading you on. Whatever that power of yours is, I'm sure it is very appealing to my son. Whatever you think is going on between the two of you, I'm sure will be cleared up when he arrives. You will see for yourself what his true nature is."

Almost on cue, the sound of cars revving up the drive blared through the windows. There was celebratory gunfire and shouting. La Madre stood up and tauntingly said, "Shall we," as she held her hand out toward the front door.

La Madre opened the front door but stood in front of it so Danika could only look out over her shoulder, which she did. She watched Javier jump out of a jeep with a machine gun strapped across his chest. Men from the other jeeps pulled five other men out of a canvas covered truck. The men had hoods over their heads and their hands were tied in front of them. The men who were taking orders from Javier were shouting and yelling; some were celebrating and others were yelling at the captives. Javier's men lined the hooded men up on the dirt path that led to the house. They had them kneel down facing the front door where La madre was standing and Dani was watching from the hallway, unseen. Once they were set up, Javier started with the first man by removing the hood. Unknown to Danika, because she was too frozen by the thought of what she was about to witness, Javier got a small nod of confirmation from La Madre then proceeded to slit the man's throat with a very large knife. He then continued down the line, receiving the okay before cutting each throat. When the last one was done all the men started shouting in celebration. Javier was covered in blood and had the look of a wild animal that just finished its prey. His eyes were cold. A pretty young girl ran up to him and gave him a towel to wipe his blood drenched face with. Once he did this he grabbed the girl and kissed her, savagely. The men dragged the bodies away leaving a trail of blood in the sand. Once Javier was done with the girl he looked over to his mother for her approval of the job done. La Madre stepped aside leaving Danika exposed in the doorway. Javier looked as if he had seen a ghost. Dani walked down the stairs as Javier ran to try and stop her.

"Don't touch me," she growled.

"Why are you here?" was all he could think to say.

"I'm asking myself the same question. I thought I was coming to find the man I love. Instead I just found out that he never really existed."

"Danika; stop," he said as he tried to grab her arm as she was about to storm away.

"Don't touch me," she hissed and sent him flying across the driveway. She tossed every man that was in her way then flung open the gates and disappeared down the path. A storm of wind was left in her wake and everyone ran for shelter; everyone except Javier. He stood on the path realizing that there was no way that she just drugged him into hallucinations and that what he just witnessed was proof that she was what she said she was. She was not an escaped homicidal maniac like that fake F.B.I agent made him believe. She was a witch. There was no doubt about it. How could he have been so stupid, he thought as the winds whipped against his body, almost feeling like her fists pounding on him. He turned around to see his mother watching him, smiling a victorious smile, then she slipped back into the house.

27

Danika was nothing but raw emotion. She ran into the jungle of thick trees. She ran and ran. She wanted to fly away but that was not going to happen. Flight only came with feelings of joy. She was running in the blinding darkness of the jungle being guided only by instinct or perhaps by the rainforest itself. She was crying. She was screaming. She was running into oblivion; somewhere where her pain would stop. She had no idea that betrayal could bring such agony. He really wasn't who she thought he was. She had fooled herself into believing that he was a victim, forced to do the things he did. That was not what she witnessed today. He could have shot those men quickly but, no; he took a knife to their throats and slit them almost as if putting on a show. The blood that poured over him had no effect on him. He was an animal reveling in his kills. He kissed that girl with brutality and it scared her. He was celebrating it all. It was to much. She thought that she could look beyond what he had been doing with his life because, maybe by being with her, he could stop. There it is; you cannot change someone, she thought. He would have to want to change, but how does someone walk away from a life born in violence. He left her easily enough to come back to this. She thought she knew him but she had not seen him in his element. Today she saw him as the killer he really was. Yet, her desire for him would not leave her and that, she realized, is where the real pain was coming from.

She came to the edge of the jungle and into a clearing. To her amazement she stood in the presence of a Mayan pyramid. She could feel it drawing her to it. With what strength she had left she ran to it. It was night and the sky was sparkling clear. The stars were like crystals. The heat of the jungle burned through her and she ripped off her clothes. The feeling of the humidity on her skin instead of the stifling cloth was relief. She kept running.

After two miles, Danika finally came to the foot of the pyramid. Her head felt like it would explode. She wanted no more thoughts. She wanted to climb the stairs to the top, to touch the stars, to fly into them and never return but she could barely walk another foot. She went to the nearest landing of the giant stone structure and laid herself down on her back. Danika stared into the night sky and began to clear her mind. She drifted into sleep and into ancient visions. She saw a king on a high landing of the pyramid. The king was joined by a priest and a priestess who stood on either side of him. Above them, on the highest point of the pyramid was a god. Mayan people; men, women and children, all of their civilization, were lined up on every step of the pyramid. There was only blackness below them all. Danika was lying in the grass on the outskirts of the black hole that surrounded the pyramid. She stood up and walked towards it. She could see some kind of movement happening which seemed as if all the people were doing in unison but she couldn't make it out. As she got closer she felt as though she were walking in mud. She looked down at the grass and lifted her foot. Blood dripped from it. The grass was being drenched with it. Looking back at the pyramid, Danika could see that the people at the first step of the pyramid were having their throats cut by the people on the steps above them. The bodies then rolled into the pit of darkness which was overflowing with their blood. Then the process started over again with the next tier of people cutting the throats of the lower level. This was what Danika saw happening in unison, one step up after another. One row of people sacrificing the lower row to the god at the top. The priest and priestess chanting holy words of praise and thanks and the king watching with pride as their god was appeased. Danika could not look away no matter how hard she tried. She knelt down in the bloody grass in submission to the horror she was forced to witness. When there were no more common people and all that were left were the king, the priest and the priestess they all looked puzzled. They looked up at their god and he was not satiated. The priest walked over and took the priestess hand. They then walked over to the king and the priestess stood on the side of the king and lifted his chin up. The priest slit the king's throat and his body rolled all the way down the pyramid into the abyss. The holy couple looked up at their god. He demanded more. The two walked towards each other and slit each other's throats and rolled after the king. The god was now alone on the top of the pyramid. He wanted more. He unhinged his jaw and it began to open as wide as the pyramid which he then devoured and fell into the abyss.

Danika heard screams. She thought that it was coming from the pit, but it seemed closer than that. After a moment of trying, in vain, to block her ears with her hands, she realized that she was the one screaming. So much death. So much blood. Just when she thought that her skull would crack she witnessed a tiny leaf pop up from the grass in front of her. It grew into a bud and opened into a little white flower. The sight of the delicate white petals filled her with bliss. Danika fell softly back onto the green grass and was once again, absent from thought.

28

Javier watched her walk away and braced himself against the wake of her hurricane. What had he done, he thought to himself as he stood there, paralyzed. She was who she said she was. There was no way she drugged him today like that so called F.B.I. agent had said. He just witnessed her power and it was amazing. She was amazing and he let her slip through his fingers. A very bad thought came to him. She has seen Dani. She also witnessed her power. He felt sick. The girl with the towel came over and put her arm on his.

"Are you okay, Javi?" she asked

"Alejandra, you need to leave here. I don't know why you hang around this hell hole," he answered and pushed past her and stormed into the house. She followed behind him.

La Madre was reclining on a chaise lounge next to the indoor pool, strategically placing herself where Javier would have to walk by her to get to the stairway to the bedrooms.

"So that is who you ran away with. What an extraordinary asset she will be to my empire. I can actually forgive you now for disappearing on us. You should have just told me you were acquiring a weapon for me."

"She has nothing to do with you. You do not go near her, do you hear me?" Javier said in the most menacing tone he could muster under the circumstance. He had never told her, no, before.

"Alejandra, come here, my dear," said La Madre.

Javier had turned to see that the pretty, young girl had followed him into the house. He should have known, seeing that she followed him everywhere. But, this wasn't good. She just witnessed his defiance. Alejandra walked over to his mother. She took her hand and helped her up from the chaise, not that she needed help. La Madre took the girl's arm in hers and walked her over to the pool.

"Alejandra, can you believe the way my son has just spoken to me? No one denies me, is that not so Alejandra?"

"No, Madre," answered the girl. They stopped at the edge of the pool and La Madre turned to her and ran one of her long red painted nails through a curl of the girl's hair. Javier began to sweat and feel nauseous and he could not move.

"How old are you now, Alejandra?" she asked.

"Eighteen, Madre,"

"You have grown into a beautiful young lady. I remember the day you were born," La Madre crooned and slowly lifted her eyes to look directly at Javier. The complete lack of color in his face was all she needed to see to know that she was having the effect that she wanted, not that she had any doubt that she would. "You have followed my son around ever since. You have been so loyal to my family. Javier, after you deliver that creature to me, you will have Alejandra for a wife, would you like that my dear?"

"Oh Madre, it would be a dream come true," the young girl said, looking over to Javier and giving him a beautiful smile.

La Madre grabbed her by the back of her neck and slammed her down on the ground and held her head in the pool. The girl was flailing but had no way to get up as La Madre put all her weight on her. La Madre knew exactly how to do this; she was an expert.

"Well, Javier? Do I send this bitch to her brother in the well? Oh, I'm sorry, I thought you had some newly developed courage. Where did it go? Don't ever think for one second that I don't have one hundred ways to cause you degrees of pain that you can't even imagine. Since you were born, I've laid in bed at night just thinking of ways to hurt you. The day you do not do my bidding is the day I release hellfire on you and you will beg to die. You know, Javier. You know this is the truth. I made you, to serve me and that's what you will do. You know you are good for nothing else. Now, go get my weapon and make her understand that she works for me now. Take this one with you," she said as she pulled Alejandra from the pool, choking for air and sobbing, " She's with the sister's."

La Madre stood up, shook the water off her hands and walked away, high heels clicking against the marble floor. "Javi," cried Alejandra and snapped him out of his frozen terror. He had just been transported back to his ten year old, helpless, terrified self, by his mother, in the way that only she knew how to do. He ran over to the girl and knelt by her side and held her as she trembled and sobbed. He soon realized that he was doing the same.

29

Danika awoke at the bottom ledge of the pyramid where she remembered being the night before. It was early morning and the sun was rising. The front of the pyramid glowed pink. She sat up and dangled her legs over the edge of the stone. She looked down at her legs and noticed that they were all cut up from her sprint through the jungle. Yesterday's events came back to her, as well as the horrible dream she had. She tried to keep those thoughts at bay as she watched the sunrise.

"Was all of the dream so horrible," asked a very small man who was sitting next to Danika. He handed her a tiny white flower like the one from her dream.

"Thank you," Dani whispered, "I guess this little piece of beauty existed there so it wasn't a hundred percent bad; just ninety nine."

"Sometimes it feels that those are the percentages of the world, does it not? Fortunately, the one percent that is good and pure exists. When you find it you must cherish it. That one percent far outweighs the ninety nine percent of bad. That one percent has kept mankind in existence. You must not lose hope, Danika, for hope is one of the greatest of all magic, is it not?"

"Who are you," Danika asked

"I am Itzamna. This is my temple," said the little man as he hopped up and walked over to an iguana who was sitting on a pile of eggs and he pet her.

"Ugh, are you a god? I'm not in the mood," said Dani in a very rude tone.

"No, my dear girl. I just built this temple, and I did it in one night as well. I am just a magical creature like yourself. I have been here for a very long time. I am of this earth, sort of like your Greenman, but I do not consider myself a god. I don't need to be worshiped to survive. I don't need anything from the human race. I just sit and watch the things they do. Some good, a lot bad," he handed her a handful of gooseberries to eat. "There is much killing here in this land. It has become a way of life. Small people come from nothing and find easy ways to become big and that usually consists of cutting down someone else. Other countries are more streamlined. Their people are occupied with possessions while the powerful cut each other down for more power. This is why we must hide our powers. Imagine if they knew what we could do."

"These gooseberries are delicious but you are making my headache come back," Dani groaned, trying to figure out where this sermon was going.

"Ah, I digress. I just wanted to tell you that your work here is not done."

"It is as far as I'm concerned. I'm on the first tour bus out of here. This place is too brutal for me. I'm going back to my forest in England."

"I am asking you to stay. Please do not give up. You have the power to stop many future deaths and to avenge past ones. You can restore balance in this land. Are you so heartless as to have that power and not use it to bring balance. You of all creatures should know the importance of balance." Itzamna had his small hands clasped together under his chin as he pleaded with her and gave her his most pathetic pout.

"Fine! What am I supposed to do, then?"

"Head down that path," he pointed to a small opening in the jungle at the edge of the clearing, " in a few miles you will find the three sisters. They will guide you. Very simple. You should get some rest before you go. I will leave you now," he said as he walked back to the iguana. He lifted her up and took one of the eggs from beneath her. It was very large. He carried it back over to Dani. "It is said that I hatched from one of these eggs. Perhaps that accounts for my size. It is neither here nor there for I am the great magician and I built this pyramid in one night," he shouted. You, my girl, are not much bigger than me but you will restore balance and bring peace to many of my people and your little one grows in your tummy, not in an egg. She will be big." He said this then touched his finger to her forehead and she fell asleep.

30

"Hellooo. Oh sista, please, you need to get up and put something on before my whole tour group comes around the corner and sees you!"

Danika woke up for the second time under the pyramid. She felt very rested but a bit confused.

"Who are you, are you with the magician?" she asked the stranger.

"Oh boy, I think somebody's been roofied! I'm Marc Le Fox and oh my god, you're British. I think I've been looking for you. But you seriously need to put some clothes on, where are they?" Marc asked as he helped her get up. He strategically placed her hair so she was covered up.

"I think they are in the jungle somewhere," Dani answered, once again trying to make sense of what was going on.

"You did have a wild night, didn't you? Here, take my scarf. It's extra big and should fit around you like a sari." Marc covered her up and tucked the fabric here and there and actually made it look like it was meant to be a dress. Dani thought to conjure up some clothes but didn't want to scare the nice man. He was very handsome with gorgeous curly, ginger hair. He wore a short beard, sunglasses and a black

Boston Red Sox's baseball hat. He was a tourist here in the Yucatan, on a tour of the Mayan temples.

"What did you mean, you are looking for me?"

"Well, I am a very experienced medium, perhaps you have heard of me?" Dani shook her head. "No, okay, whatever. I usually get messages from the deceased to give to their loved ones. However, on my way here, on the plane I started getting really loud messages and it turns out they are loud because they are from the living. Do you know someone named AnneMarie?"

"Yes!" Dani answered.

"Well, she's a pain in my ass. She's talking right now as a matter of fact. She says that you need to open a door like the one you made for her. Then you need to use the book. Make sure you open the door. You will know when. Don't you bitches have cell phones.?"

"Witches, not bitches and we don't use cell phones. Electromagnetic static disrupts our energy."

"Huh," was all he had to say to that.

"Why couldn't she contact me herself?" Dani asked.

"She tried but there are wards being put up all around you. She says to be careful and trust your heart, aaaw that's nice. Are we done here? My chauffeur, William, is probably looking for me. He's not happy unless I'm bossing him around. Do you need a ride?"

"No, I know where I'm going. Thank you so much for your help, you are very sweet." She kissed his cheek.

"Yeah, well , don't spread it around. Oh here's a pair of flip flops; they go with the scarf. You'll need them if you're walking. Good luck."

With that, Danika and Marc parted ways and she walked onto the path and into the jungle.

31

It was a short mile walk down the path, through the jungle, just like Itzamna had said. Dani came to a clearing and saw a small farmhouse with a porch. There were chickens running around the yard and two burrows grazing on grass. A few yards in front of the house were two women in rocking chairs sitting around a low burning fire that had a grate over it and a pot of something on it. A third woman came slowly out of the house and down the stairs of the porch. She was carrying a tray that had on it what looked like breakfast. She walked up to Danika.

"Here, take this for me. My grip isn't what it used to be. I'm sorry but we don't have tea, just coffee. Come." said the woman as she led Dani over to the other women by the fire. She sat in her rocker. There were four plates of eggs, rice and beans and some papaya. Dani served each of the ladies then sat over near the one who brought the tray and was now pouring coffee. She passed the cups around the circle.

Dani was starving. She started to remember her visit with Itzamna and the gooseberries he had given her. This meal looked much heartier.

"Do you ladies know Itzamna?" Dani had to ask.

"Of course we do. He is the magician. He built our temple," Maria answered

"Did he visit you?" Izchel asked excitedly, "Did he show you the egg?"

Dani had her face in her dish but stopped abruptly and looked up slowly from her bowl as she remembered, just at that moment, what he had said about her tummy. She looked at each of the sisters as they eagerly waited for a response that she was almost afraid to give. Dani gulped the bite of food that was in her mouth.

"Yes."

"Oooo, I knew it!" shouted Lucia as she flew back in her rocking chair clapping her hands.

"You are going to have a mighty little magician on your hands. Between your powers and that granted by Itzamna, and the strength and cunning of the wolf, very powerful," said Maria, "La Madre should never lay eyes on her, if you know what's good for you. I wonder if you do know what's good for you, seeing as how you walked into her house and paraded yourself in front of her. Didn't el Lobo warn you?"

"Ladies, you are making my head spin. I'm trying to keep up with the things that you are throwing at me but I had a really rough night and I'm a little slow on the uptake. May I please have some coffee, and what do you know about the Wolf?" Dani asked, stretching over the fire to grab the pot of coffee and pouring some into a cup.

"We know that he is walking down the path behind you with our niece," answered Lucia, with a bit of a giggle in her tone.

Danika, once again, gulped down the contents of her mouth, which she thought was more lady like than spitting it out. She stood up, straightened her scarf dress then turned to face him. He was walking down the path that had led her here. How did he know where she was?

He, also, had his pretty little girlfriend from the other day, with him. Did they say she was their niece? She was a lot younger looking today than yesterday; she's just a kid. The girl had run ahead of Javier. She walked by Danika and they, sort of, summed each other up. She ran over to her aunts and greeted each of them with hugs and kisses and there was some commotion about the bruises on her neck, but Dani didn't catch any of it because Javier was standing right in front of her and she could smell the scent of his skin mixed with the humidity and the air and it was delicious. She finally got herself to look up at him.

"We need to talk," was all he said, and started walking.

32

She followed him away from the house and into the trees. When they were far enough away where they would not be heard he turned around to face her. He pulled her to him and kissed her. He kissed her so hard she thought her lips would bleed. But, it wasn't violent like she had seen him do to the girl; it was desperate. He kissed her face and her neck and her chest. His arms were like a vice grip. She thought for one, tiny, little moment to stop him but that moment flitted away. He picked her up and she wrapped her legs around him and he eased her to the ground. He was inside her in a second. He began thrusting into her as if his life depended on it. She bit into his shoulder trying not to let out the screams of pleasure that were welling up inside her. He slid his arms underneath her and pulled her up so he could go even deeper, her legs gripping him and pushing him in assistance. Harder and deeper until there was no more space between them and they could each feel nothing but the heat and the massive pressure of the other. Then, release; and, an ear splitting howl that was responded to by nearby wolves.

He laid on top of her for a few moments then sat up. He scooped her up and held her in his arms and kissed her neck and shoulders.

"I am so sorry. I don't have any right to ask for your forgiveness. I left you in trouble. I let a complete stranger trick me into believing you were not what you said you were. I chose to believe the lie that was fed to me. The only thing I can say in my defense is that I believed the lie because I really thought that you were too good for me. After all the bad I have done in my life, how could I deserve someone so good. I don't believe that I deserve happiness. Every minute I'm with you I fear that she will find a way to take you from me and I won't be able to bear that. So, I took the opportunity that idiot gave me and I ran. I didn't stop for a second, I just ran back here and realized that she was in my head and I will never be free of her. I'm still trying to figure out if she set that whole thing up."

"She didn't. It was a cult thing, but I'm not going to get into that now. I can totally see how you could believe the worst.During my short visit with Suzanna, I recognized right away what a master manipulator she is. Even with that awareness she still tricked me. She made sure I was in the right place to see your display yesterday. She bet on the fact that the sight of what you were going to do; what you did, would send me running. She was right, wasn't she?"

"Do you hate me after seeing what I really am?"

"I love you. I could never hate you. Today proved that. But, I cannot be with you if you don't stop. My whole world is about creation, not destruction. I do not believe that this is the life that was meant for you. If I asked you to walk away from her and never take another order from her again, will you?"

"That has been my plan since the day we met on the bus. But, we have a problem. She knows you now. She has seen what you can do. I have been ordered to bring you to her and advise you that you now work for her," Javier said in a dead, serious tone.

Danika, who had been lying against his chest and was wrapped in his arms, turned her head to look up at him. She met his serious gaze; then burst out in laughter. He gently slid out from under her, stood up and brushed himself off. He started to pace a little with his elbows out and his hands above his head.

"You can't possibly think that she can harm me! I walked right into her nest yesterday just to prove to her that she can't hurt me. I rendered her and all her men powerless. Not to mention the fact that I can't be killed," Dani said, and regretted it the second she did.

"What do you mean you can't be killed?" Javier asked, incredulously.

"Where I come from, for my coven and many others, I am an Archive. I was chosen to carry ancient knowledge that has been collected since the beginning of time. As long as it is carried we can all access it. It's like a huge library in the recesses of my mind. I had power that was brought to the surface by practicing the craft but the Archive makes me even more powerful. It's like everything is at the surface for me, ready to use. Some witches have to plan their spells or work for days on potions but for me it's almost instant. Anyway, being an Archive means I will live for about three hundred years. I'm only twenty five at the moment. She can't kill me."

"Dani, she doesn't control people by hurting them, she hurts everyone around them. I told you why I took painstaking precautions to protect Jose. Everytime I stepped out of line she killed someone that was even remotely close to me. Even if you don't think there's anyone left, she will find someone you hadn't thought of. After the display you put on for her yesterday, she is going to be obsessed with your powers. I don't know what she is planning but she wouldn't have sent me to get you if she didn't have someone to leverage. I'm sick to think of what she is planning."

"Javi, she has no power over me and she can't kill me. You are the only one here that I love and she's not going to kill you."

"Why not?" he asked with that face, again. Danika realized that he was really serious.

"Because if she killed you then she really wouldn't have anything to bargain with would she."

"Dani, you are not understanding how she works, she doesn't have to kill me. She might torture me in front of you till you broke. That's probably what she has planned."

"You know what, screw this! I'm sick of all of it. The sooner we face off the better. At this point, I'm itching for a scrap. The madder she makes me the more hurt I'll rain down on her," Dani stood up and brushed some grass off herself and adjusted her scarf dress. Then she decided she wasn't going to a fight wrapped in a scarf. She bent over and touched the tips of her toes and as she rose up her clothes were transformed to black hiking boots, black cargo pants and a black tank top. The gray scarf was on the ground and she picked it up and wrapped it around her neck. Now, she was ready for battle.

They walked back to the house. The sisters had gone onto the porch for some shade and were rocking on their chairs there. When they saw the couple coming back they came to meet them.

"Are you children going to see La Madre?" asked Maria?

"Yes, auntie, did you need something? Javier asked in return.

"Alejandra told us that La Madre wanted to see us at her house and then she ran ahead. Can we get a ride?"

The instincts that had kept Javier alive all these years were sounding the alarm. Danika was feeling the same way. They couldn't figure how the three sisters could be part of this. Perhaps she thought that she could get them to use their magic against Danika. Once again, Dani wanted to stop overthinking everything and get this over with. This, Dani laughed to herself, was why she wasn't a very good chess player.

"Let go," she said to Javier. He ran to the path where the jeep was parked and pulled it up to the house. The five of them got in the vehicle and rolled down the path and into the jungle.

33

It was a straight path through the forest from the house of the three sisters' to La Madre's hacienda. El Adivino was right in the middle of that path and that is where La Madre set her trap. As Javier, Danika and the sisters came out of the jungle in the jeep, they were stopped by men with machine guns who were lined up across the path. Javier looked in the rearview mirror and saw more come out of the jungle and line up behind them. The men, who were usually led by Javier, pulled Danika and Javier from the jeep and had them walk ahead, while one of the men got in and drove the jeep with the old women behind them. They were being led to the front of the massive pyramid where Dani had slept the night before. She started to remember the dream she had that night and thought to herself, that more blood may be about to pour on these grounds. There were more men and more guns and La Madre stood behind them all on the stone platform at the base of El Adivino.

"Javier, my son, now is not the time to try to be brave, so put any thoughts of it out of your mind. You know better than anyone that I will get what I want. Have you discussed that with the young lady?" asked La Madre with a threat in her voice.

"Why would she submit to your demands? There is nothing you can do to any of us. You can't shoot us. She won't let that happen. You saw the power she has and it is hers alone. She and I are walking out of here today and I am leaving this country with her. Send the sisters home, there is no reason for them to be here. You have made them and their whole family suffer enough."

"I have seen her power and it will be the greatest asset to our business. You have done well by finding this rare jewel. The sisters are not going anywhere because they are about to perform a binding ritual, right here at their sacred temple," said La Madre and moved her dead stare from Javier to Danika just in time to see the flash of panic in her eyes. Danika quickly centered herself.

"Why on earth would I allow a binding spell to happen? I think you should quit while you're ahead and do as Javier said and then we can all be back to our own business."

"My son is my business. Everything about him is my business. There is nothing he can hide from me," she said menacingly, looking back over to Javier to see if he got her meaning.

His knees buckled and he almost fell to the ground but Dani held him up.

"What is it?" Dani asked him, seeing that all the color had drained from his face.

La Madre put her arm out to the side with her palm open. From out of an alcove of the pyramid came Valentina, Alejandra's mother and the three sisters' niece; the mother of the boy in the well. She handed La Madre a walkie talkie. She tossed it to Javier.

"Jose?" he asked, praying he was wrong.

"Javi, I tried to keep them out, I ran to the panic room but I wasn't fast enough. I'm sorry," said Jose.

"Listen, kid, you have nothing to be sorry for. This is not your fault. I will get you out of this. Just stay calm and do what they say. How many men are with you?" With that one of the armed men grabbed the walkie talkie from Javier and gave it back to La Madre. Javier looked at Dani. He was pleading for her to do something with his eyes. The pain Dani saw in them was breaking her heart. She would not let this happen. She closed her eyes and searched for Jose. If she could locate him in her mind she could transport him somewhere else. Nothing. She tried again. Again, nothing, she could not locate him.

"You are not the only bruja here, Danika. Valentina has improved her skills over the years; as hard as that was with the state of her. She has placed wards where they need to be to prevent you from using your mind to receive messages or to look beyond. You will not be able to locate my grandson."

"Don't call him that," Javier hissed.

"Valentina, what have you done?" cried Maria, "How could you help her after all she has put us through; after what she has done to you? She will destroy us all!"

"What difference does it make," answered Valentina, with no emotion left, "I was destroyed a long time ago. El Lobo was supposed to bring help from the house of light from across the sea but all the while he killed at her bidding. I have waited to long for revenge that isn't coming. My surviving child is just another pawn in their game awaiting slaughter and there's nothing I can do but sit and wait for that agony to come. No, I just assume to let her kill us all and get it over with. I've been dead since the day she killed my son. I am giving her what she wants so we can all have a quick death."

The sisters were in shock. They looked at Danika. Three more sets of pleading eyes. Danika had to do some quick thinking.

"So, Suzanna," Dani said in the most confident voice she could muster, "your plan is to make the sisters do a binding spell that will bind my powers to you, is that right?"

"Yes, my dear. If you do not agree to this then I will have my grandson killed, slowly. You know how it's done, don't you Javier?"

"I have a suggestion that may interest you more. What if you were able to have your own power and not have to use me as a middle man? I have acquired a book of extreme power, more power than I have. I am not allowed to use it, unfortunately, I am bound to keep it in my archive only. If I were to give you this book you could wield your own power. I mean, if something happened to me, you would be back where you started, and once you've tasted supernatural power, it's very hard to live without it."

"What is this book called?" asked La Madre, her interest piqued.

"The Necronomicon," answered Danika. La Madre looked at Valentina for confirmation.

"I have heard whispers of this book. It is the book of the dead and supposedly contains great knowledge and power for the one who reads from it," Valentina confirmed. The fact that she didn't know more about the book was what Dani had been hoping for.

"What do you expect in return?" she asked, skeptically.

"You will let Jose, Javier and myself go free. You will have no need of the sisters, so you should let them go about their business."

"Everyone but Javier. I will never let him go. If you accept those terms we can begin the trade."

Danika looked at Javier but already knew what his answer would be before he gave it.

"Get him away from her. If you love me, you must do this for me."

"I will," she said with tears in her eyes and she threw her arms around him and they held each other. She let him go then turned to La Madre.

"Agreed."

"I like the way you do business, my dear. Shall we begin."

34

Danika left Javier's side and climbed the stairs to the platform next to La Madre.

"No tricks or Valentina will give the word and that boy's slow death begins. So, what do we do?"

"I will summon the book and give it to you. When you read from it you will unleash its power and you will reap its rewards, it's that simple."

"And why have you not used this book yourself?" asked La Madre who was salivating at the thought of having her own supernatural power on top of her own power of fear and violence.

"My coven has entrusted me to keep powerful objects in a library inside my mind. I am supposed to keep them, not use them. You are making me break the trust of my coven and I'll probably be banished but I am willing to do this to save his son. How do I know you will keep your word?" Dani asked in return.

"Ask Javier. My word is good." Danika looked down at Javier who stood with the others in the grass. He nodded in agreement.

Danika bent her head and held out her hands. A red light surrounded them as the book was brought forth. She handed it to La

Madre who immediately began to stroke the skin that the binding was made of. She walked over to a standing stone and placed the book on it, without losing contact with it. Danika could see the book influencing her already. La Madre opened it and caressed the pages. She touched the written words with her finger and then touched it to her tongue and tasted the blood of the ink that was as fresh as the days it was written. The pages began to glow red and she began to read aloud.

"Hear me all who lie in the ground for I am the Queen of chaos!" The words she read appeared as she read them. The words seemed to appear especially for the reader. She could feel power surge through and she reveled in it. "I call forth my army to do my bidding! Souls bound to the earth come forth and bring your power. Hear me for I am your queen, your judge, you executioner. I live by the sword of power and corruption and I wield it through you all! Come to me, all powerful ones and put me on my throne so you may carry me to my rightful place among you! Be restless no more, my army, for I am here to collect my glory and rule you all!"

With that, the ground began to shake. All the men with guns began to look around trying to decide whether to stay or flee. Danika closed her eyes and went deep into her mind. She imagined a door. It was red with a gold knob. She watched the door. After a few moments she heard a knock. It was ready. Dani opened her eyes and looked to where Valentina was standing with Alejandra. Dani raised her hand and conjured the door behind them. There was another knock. La Madre, at her podium, glowed red with light from the book that was unleashing its power. Another knock at the door. The men on the ground started to jump and shoot at the ground. Hands were digging through the earth and heads were coming up behind them. Most of the men began to run. There were bodies crawling from the grass and walking towards La Madre.

"Come to me, my children! I am your queen," she yelled in triumph.

Valentina turned to look at the door. The knocking from the door was pounding through her head. In all the chaos, this was all she could hear. She ran to the door and threw it open. Her little son walked through the door and took her hand. Valentina dropped the walkie talkie.

"I"ve missed you so much, mama. Come home with me," he said. She picked up her son with tears streaming from her eyes and walked back through the door. The door vanished. Alejandra screamed when she saw the door disappear. Danika ran over and grabbed her.

"She's gone. She's with your brother now and her suffering is over. Don't worry, I'll keep you safe. Come with me!" Danika took her hand and they ran down the steps to Javier and the sisters. Danika told Javier that Jose was safe and handed him the walkie talkie that Valentina had left behind. Alejandra ran to her aunts who held her as she cried.

"That is right, my children! Come to me! I am your queen. Give me the power!" shouted La Madre as her army approached. They were climbing up the short wall in front of her, moaning. She could see them clearly now. They were corpses, but not just any corpses. She saw her husband and her son Gabriel. She was overjoyed. The power of the book was granting her, her every wish. Then she saw Don Pascal, with a bloody hole in his head. She saw two young ladies that Javier had been with, one's head was barely on her shoulders because her throat had been slit so deep. Javier's nanny crawled towards her with her head bashed in. She began to recognize one after another. Just at the moment that she realized that her army was, actually, all of her victims, her son Gabriel grabbed her ankle and pulled. Don Pascal grabbed the other ankle and pulled as well. She fell to the hard stone. More corpses grabbed her and dragged her from the stone landing and onto the grass. They dragged her past Javier and she screamed at him to stop them.

He closed his eyes and turned his head away. There were hundreds of corpses that had risen from the earth. They had been set free to take their revenge on the creature who had taken their lives. They had come to drag La Madre to hell. This was the gift the Necronomicon had for LaMadre. The corpses surrounded her and dragged her into the earth with them. Then, silence.

The only ones left were Javier, Danika, Alejandra and the three sisters. Javier picked up the walkie talkie.

"This is the Wolf. La Madre is dead. Let me speak to the boy."

"Dad?" said Jose.

"She told you?" asked Javier with a tear rolling down his cheek.

"No. I always knew. What kind of guy hangs around a kid all the time? I figured you were either my father or a pervert and you were too cool to be a pervert. Can you tell these assholes to fuck off?"

"Bring my son to the hacienda. Out."

"Yes, boss," replied one of the men.

"We are bringing Alejandra home with us. She has been through too much for such a young girl," said Izchel.

"Lobo, before you leave us, bring your lady back to our home. We have something to discuss with the both of you once we have all settled down," said Maria. Lucia just pushed Javier out of the way and hugged Danika.

The sisters piled in the jeep and Alejandra drove them back down the path to their house. Javier and Danika got into another jeep and began down the path to the hacienda. A few seconds later, they backed up and drove to the foot of the temple. Dani jumped out of the jeep and ran up the stairs to the landing. There was the Necronomicon, lying on the cold stone doing its best to look sweet and innocent.

"Oh no you don't," said Dani as she picked up the book and returned it to the Archive. She jumped off the landing and into the jeep and turned to Javier. "That would not have been good." They drove away from El Adivino and back to the hacienda.

35

Three white jeeps rolled past the gates and down the path of the hacienda. They pulled up to the front of the large house. Armed men jumped out of the vehicles. The boss got out of the second jeep. He lit a cigar as he surveyed the scene. He turned to his guard.

"What the hell is going on here? Where the hell is everybody?"

"I don't know, boss. There is no one anywhere on the grounds."

The boss walked up the stairs and opened the large double doors of the hacienda. He walked down the large foyer. He could hear muffled shooting coming from the pool room. He drew his gun and walked slowly into the room. There was a large T.V. on and there was a video game on the screen. The boss saw the top of someone's head on the couch in front of the television. He walked slowly around the couch to see who it was, weapon drawn and ready.

"Who the hell are you?" he asked the person on the couch.

"Who the hell are you?" the young man playing the game retorted, completely unimpressed by the man who was pointing a very large gun at him.

"I am Francisco. Where is La Madre? Where is Javier? Where is anyone? And you better tell me who you are or I'm going to blow your head off," said Francisco, not used to being spoken back to.

The boy struggled through an attack on his game. There was an explosion and he threw the controls down on the coffee table that was full of snacks, soft drinks and beers. Things flew off the table.

"Fuck! That bitch is dead, Javier's upstairs messing around with his old lady and I'm your nephew, Jose. Are we done?" He picked the controls up and started a new game.

Francisco stood there in disbelief for a minute. He decided he was not going to get any straight answers from… his nephew? He turned around and out the door and up the stairs. He heard moaning coming from Javier's room. He knocked on the door. Louder moaning. He knocked again. A noise, he wasn't sure what it was. Francisco stood there a moment and then the door opened. Javier slid out of the door in his bikini underwear.

"Javi, what the hell is going on? Where is everyone?"

"Tio, I am so happy to see you!" Javier said as he grabbed his uncle and hugged him. "My mother is dead! I have a son and I have, what will soon be my wife. Things couldn't be better. Oh, wait one minute." Javier slipped back into the room then out again. He handed his uncle a set of keys. "Here you are, tio, the keys to the kingdom. I'm leaving and La Madre's empire and the hacienda are all yours. I'm done. I'm out. I'm in love. I have a real family. I love you, tio but I don't think I will be seeing you again after today."

"You are serious. Where are you going?" his uncle asked in disbelief.

"I'm not telling anyone. I want to have a clean break, a fresh start. You know I have never wanted this life and I have a chance to be free of it and I'm going to take it. And you, tio, you were born for it. You are now, Don Francisco Arturo."

There was a noise from behind them. Francisco drew his gun and spun around. It was a man with a large box. Javier put his hand on his uncle's and had him lower his weapon. Javier was grinning his famous tight lipped grin.

"Is that it?" he asked the man.

"Si senor," answered the man.

Javier hugged his uncle again then ran past him and grabbed the box.

"Gracias," he said as he took it. "Tio, give him something, I have no pockets," and he headed back to the room. "Adios, tio."

In the bedroom, Javier put the box on the floor and pulled back the curtain.

"Rise and shine, mi amor!"

Danika lay on the bed on her stomach, covered only by strands of her long hair.

"I can't get up. I don't think I will be able to walk today. One more day and then we will leave," she groaned.

"No, no. Today is the first day of our new lives. We leave today. I have already handed over the keys to the kingdom to my uncle. I will make us breakfast, we will go see the sisters, then we go," he said as he straddled her on the bed. She turned over, beneath him, then looked up to see him looking down at her with his black, wavy hair hanging down the sides of his face. He was grinning that grin and his eyes held the joy of a child. She reached up and touched his chest, and his smooth stomach then rested them on his slender hips.

"You need to get off me. I can't take anymore," Dani said, half joking.

"One more thing. I have a surprise for you." He jumped off of the bed and picked up the box and put it next to Dani. She opened the loosely closed flaps.

"What did you do?" she asked as she pulled a fat German Shepherd puppy out of the box.

"I know he can't be replaced, but I thought we could call him Anubis Junior. I will never forgive myself for not protecting both of you that night. I hope you can forgive me someday."

"Javi, Anubis is alive. He was only tranquilized with a dart gun. He's in Lawrence, Massachusetts, being dog sat by a group of young witches who are spoiling him rotten." Javier grabbed her and hugged her, and the puppy.

"I can't tell you how happy I am to hear that. I love that dog and I know how important he is to you. What a relief. I think that has helped me make up my mind about where we should go. I want to go back there. I want to live in that house. Something there felt right; felt like home."

"I think that's a great idea, but we won't be alone. The girls will be there for a while and there will be witches coming and going," Dani said, as she looked up at him and watched his thoughts process.

"I am quite used to having a house full of people. That is fine with me. So, that is it then. We're going back to Massachusetts!"

"Hey, why don't you go downstairs and give this chubby little monster to Jose."

"Really?" Dani shook her head, yes. "Okay!" He hugged her again then grabbed the puppy and ran out the door.

"Put some clothes on," Dani yelled after him, but it was too late.

36

Francisco's men were already on their way to the hacienda. Javi, Dani and Jose passed them on the road as they headed to the three sister's farmhouse. They passed El Adivino on the way, as well. Danika looked back as they passed and she saw Itzamna high up at the temple opening. He waved to her and she heard him say, gracias and adios. She waved back.

"Who are you waving to," asked Jose as he wrestled with the puppy who tried to lick Jose's face every time he moved.

"A new friend who I probably will never see again," she answered with a bit of sadness in her voice. Javi put his hand on hers and held it.

A few minutes later they were at the farmhouse. The three sisters were rocking in their chairs around the fire and Alejandra was pouring them coffee. The travelers jumped out of the jeep and walked over to them. Alejandra ran to Javier and wrapped her arms around his waist and hugged him.

"You are leaving?" she asked him with a sad pout on her face.

"We are. I am so sorry about your mother but I know your aunts will take good care of you," he said as he stroked her hair.

"My mother has been dead since I was born. She tried but she could never get over my brother's death. She is happy now. I know this is true. My aunties are going to take very good care of me. They say I have the makings of a real bruja, like you Dani," she said, acknowledging Dani. "Javier, I have to tell you, it is my fault they found your son. La Madre sent me to follow you all the time. I'm so sorry. You were always so kind to me and my family. I don't know why we always did what she told us too. I'm not sorry that she is gone."

"None of us are," Javier said, "and I know that you followed me all the time. That's why I called you my little shadow. It's all okay now."

"Enough girl," shouted Maria, "let him go and go play with the boy and his puppy. We have things to discuss." Alejandra squeezed Javi one more time and Jose rolled his eyes at being called a boy. They walked over and sat on the porch and put the puppy down to play in the yard.

"What is his name?" Alejandra asked.

"Lobo," answered Jose. They watched the awkward little puppy try to catch the chickens.

Back at the fire, Javier and Danika sat on an old tree stump near the sisters.

"My dear Danika," Maria began, "you have done us a huge service by ridding us of La Madre. She has caused us so much suffering for many years. We could never have done it ourselves because we are all too entwined with each other. She had ways to hurt us all and we just learned to live with her, somehow. You have a good man in Javier, I think you know this. He was a pure child who was corrupted by a very bad woman. We believe he deserves a second chance. We can not send him back in time nor would you want that, but there is something else we can do."

"Danika," Izchel interjected, "we know that you must carry the load of ancient knowledge for almost three hundred years. This is a very long life and we think Javier should live it with you. It will give him a chance to do this lifetime over, to make up for the bad things that he has done. With you by his side and his growing family's love, we see him doing great things in this world."

"Is this possible?" Danika asked.

"It is our gift to you and him," answered Lucia. "Javier, this is as much a blessing as it is a burden. Three hundred years is a long time to walk the earth. But, as we said, with your soulmate by your side, you can do great things with that time."

"What about my son," Javier asked as he watched Jose chase the puppy around the yard.

"He will live his normal life. He will, however, benefit from never having to lose his parents or have to nurse them in their old age. You will have each other to console when he passes. But, this is a lifetime away and I think you understand what we are offering. Do you accept this gift?

"I don't deserve this gift, but she does. I will never leave her side. I would walk with her for eternity," Javier answered.

The three sisters stood up and walked close to each other. They stood in a circle with their pinky fingers touching. They began to cast a spell in an ancient Mayan language. They chanted louder and louder then lifted their hands to the sky. Danika and Javier looked up at the sky. The sun was high above them. Danika started to see something moving in the sky. It was a flame, a piece of the sun that they were bringing to them. The sisters controlled the flame and brought it to the firepit, like they had done with the stars. The flame, about the size of a heart now, was spinning above the firepit.

"Javier, put your hands beneath the Sacred Flame," Izchel commanded.

He did so and the flame turned to liquid and poured into his hands.

"Drink,"commanded the sisters, in unison. He did so and the liquid slid down his throat. His body was alight with the fire and life of the sun and he screamed out and fell to the ground. The light was absorbed into him and the pain stopped. The spell was cast.

37

"Javi!" Danika shouted from the kitchen as Javier had just walked in the front door, "go back out and get some firewood. Aunties are freezing to death!" Anubis went running to the door with the puppy attached to his tail. He jumped up on Javi and the puppy latched on to his pant leg.

"Dani, I've got Martin with me. Come on, man you can help me carry some wood in."

"If I must," Martin responded and they headed out the door with the dogs barking ahead of them and rolling in the snow.

In the kitchen, Danika was rolling out a pie crust. She was covered with flour and the counter looked like a bakery. Jenna and Anne Marie were helping.

"Who is Martin?" Jenna asked as she frosted some sugar cookies.

"He's the guy who kidnapped me and tried to get me to open the Necronomicon, remember? The cult leader. Anyway, he helped Javier enroll in Havard's business school. He's a professor there and he owed me a big favor. So, I paid him a visit and asked him if he would show him around. They've been friends ever since. They're like the odd couple."

"Tell me again why we are making all this food," Anne Marie said as she toasted a bagel for herself.

"It's Christmas!" Jenna exclaimed. "Javi and I wanted to celebrate the winter solstice in a very special way after everything we all have been through. He wanted me to celebrate in my pagan way and I wanted to celebrate a big Mexican Christmas for him, so we decided to split the difference and go all American. We're going to have more food than we could eat in a year and we've bought more presents than anyone will know what to do with. The girls are going to sing carols, accompanied by Jose on guitar. We have lots of eggnog and alcohol, it's snowing, the tree is twelve feet high and the house is filled to the hilt with family. What's better than that?"

Jenna and Anne Marie exchanged glances and rolled their eyes.

"I think it's hormones," Jenna said and they both giggled.

At the dinner table, the Coven sisters sat around drinking goblets of wine and catching up after being in different parts of the country. The young witches, including Liza and Alejandra were all showing off their different abilities up in the attic which they had taken over as a dorm. The three sisters were bundled up next to the fireplace and had vowed to never come to such a cold place again. Bast and Cleopatra were taking complete advantage of them, jumping from one warm lap to another, receiving an endless supply of petting. Marc Le Fox even showed up at Anne Marie's request. They had become good friends, communicating through the ether. Marc's husband had an emergency meeting in Washington and Marc was going to be alone, so he gladly accepted the invitation. Danika had given him his scarf back as a Christmas present. William, his chauffeur, got him from Providence to Lawrence in about thirty minutes; it's an hour and a half drive. Turned out that William wasn't just a chauffeur. He was actually a very wealthy man who owned a collection of race cars and took any opportunity to use them. He spent the evening flirting with Yvette and Marc was enter-taining the three sisters. Jose invited his new friend Jake, a shy, quiet kid like himself. They met at MIT where Jose had recently enrolled after having his first big argument with his father. Javier wanted Jose to go to business school with him but Jose has a passion for tech, and won he the battle. Dani figured that, if they lived this close to Boston, they were going to take advantage of the colleges, after all, she had a couple of very smart men under her roof.

The large group had eaten an amazing meal and they all went into the giant living room and were singing Christmas carols around the fire. The last song of the evening was sung by Emi, the beautiful, young witch with platinum blonde hair. She was dressed in a white angora sweater and white jeans. She looked like an angel. She proceeded to sing Silent Night, acapella. Everyone's eyes were glistening.

Javier was sitting in a large wingback chair in the corner of the room next to the Christmas tree. Danika was on his lap. He reached down the side of the chair and brought up a small, gift wrapped box. He handed it to Dani and she opened it. Inside was a metallic ornament of a yellow bus and on the front was hand painted, Merida.

"Best day of my long life," she said as she handed him a small gift wrapped box. He unwrapped it. It was a pair of pink knitted baby booties.

"Best day of my long life," he said, "I was wondering when you were going to tell me," he said, looking at her with that tight lipped grin and his smiling eyes.

"You knew?" she asked in surprise.

"I knew. All the little hints didn't get past me. We just didn't have a chance to discuss it and I wanted you to be the one to tell me. I don't deserve such happiness," he whispered to her as he kissed her hands.

"We both deserve it," she whispered back.

Danika put her head on his chest and began to fall asleep, surrounded by family, listening to the voice of an angel and watching the lights on the tree turn to little stars, then disappear as she closed her eyes.